FRANCES THOMAS was born in Wales, but has lived in London for most of her life. Some years ago, she and her historian husband moved to mid-Wales. She has written many books for adults and children. One of her ..... .ant children's novels, *Finding Minerva*, won the Tir na nOg prize in 2008, and her picture book, *Supposing*, illustrated by Ross Collins, won a Scottish Arts Council Award in 1999.

Her biography of Christina Rossetti has been recently reprinted, and she is planning to write a biography of Eleanor Farjeon. As well as writing, she worked for many years teaching dyslexic children. She has two adult daughters and two grandchildren. You can visit her website at www.francesthomas.org.

Praise for *Helen's Daughter*

'*Helen's Daughter* is a marvellous book – pacy, exciting, forboding, and filled with fascinating characters. Frances Thomas writes with a sure, light touch, bringing out to the full the beauty and tragedy of the legend. I really loved it. A fabulous introduction to the sometimes neglected beginning of the Trojan War.'
– Katherine Langrish, author of *West of the Moon*

'The sights, sounds and smells of the ancient world are captured here with a poet's skill. We are drawn irresistibly in to Hermione's world as if seeing it through her own eyes. She is a captivating heroine. I can hardly wait for the other stories in this series...'
– Sandra Horn, author of *The Silkie*

'Thrilling, original and romantic, just what an intelligent girl of eleven would love.'
– Amanda Craig, author of *Hearts and Minds*

THE
BURNING
TOWERS

✦

FRANCES THOMAS

SilverWood

Published in 2014 by SilverWood Books

SilverWood Books Ltd
30 Queen Charlotte Street, Bristol, BS1 4HJ
www.silverwoodbooks.co.uk

ISBN 978-1-78132-323-6 (paperback)
ISBN 978-1-78132-324-3 (ebook)

British Library Cataloguing in Publication Data
A CIP catalogue record for this book is available from
the British Library

Set in Sabon by SilverWood Books
Printed on responsibly sourced paper

Chapter One

'I am not a slave.'

I say this to myself every night as I look out of my little window under the eaves, in the tiny closet next to my mistress's room.

But I *am* a slave. Saying the opposite doesn't make any difference.

If I stand on tiptoe and squint, I can just about see the sea. Or at least I think I can see its reflection against the sky. I remember how I used to go down to the shore in the old days and just stand there on the white sand for hours looking and looking at the silvery glitter of the wave tips, and the deep turquoise of the horizon. I used to wonder whether Poseidon was looking out at me; I used to imagine that I'd see his gleaming chariot rising out of the waves, drawn by four white horses, shaking drops of water from his trident.

Only it wasn't Poseidon that came out of the sea for me that day.

My mother warned me, of course, but I wouldn't listen. I loved to go down to that rocky beach, take off my sandals and let the scribble of foam wash over my toes, as I jumped in and out of the waves.

I'm not a slave! But the men who came out of the sea that day made me one, and nothing I can say now will make any difference.

Yet I say it in my own language. I say it to keep myself alive.

It's morning, and soon I have to go and get my mistress ready for the temple. At first I had no idea how to do the things I had to do – arrange her hair and dress her. One of the old slave women taught me, and now Madam prefers me to anyone else.

It takes me time to get prepared. First I have to go downstairs and across the courtyard to the kitchens to collect a kettleful of hot coals. When they're exactly the right shade of greyish-red, I shall plunge the curling tongs in, then take them out to cool. We can't have Madam's forehead burned!

Meanwhile, I assemble her priestess robes. I took them out of the chest last night and hung them over a chair so all the creases came out. They're old-fashioned and heavy. Once, while she was still asleep, I tried them on. I thought they fitted me better than they fitted her: she's grown tall in the last year and new clothes are not to be had at the moment. I tried to snatch a glance at myself in the mirror, but I was frightened in case she woke up and I got a beating. There's a skirt, tied at the waist, made up of tiers of linen, each layer stiff with embroidery and edged with a gold fringe. Then there's a bodice with sleeves to the elbow, done up at the back with tiny bows. Then there are gold sandals to complete her finery.

Next the hair. I have to use the curling tongs to make five little curls, which I stick on to her forehead with a special starchy liquid. Then I create the two long side curls. I position the silver diadem so that the long curls hang down. The rest of her hair has been woven overnight in tight little plaits – when I undo them, her hair should ripple down her back. Cassandra's hair is fine and slippery, dark blonde and hard work. Mine is thick and curly – it would take someone half the time and effort to do it to mine.

But I'm not a priestess of Apollo, as Madam keeps reminding me. I don't need my hair dressed. I couldn't dress it anyway. It bushes around my face in a mass of tight little dark curls, which I can see sometimes when I sneak a look in Cassandra's polished mirror. We slaves have our hair cut short so everyone can see what we are. (At least all of us do apart from the slaves who serve our Lady Helen. She likes to have pretty girls around her, knowing that however pretty they are, she'll always outshine them. Lady Helen always seems to get her own way in everything.)

My mistress is still asleep. Cassandra sleeps very heavily, like someone dead. She says she has extraordinary dreams. At any rate, she seems to be in another world when she sleeps, with her plaits snaking wildly over the pillow like Medusa's hair, and her little mouth slightly open and (dare I say it?) snoring faintly. You can't see her eyes – they're her best feature – long and almond-shaped, a kind of silvery grey with winged brows. All you can see now are long lashes curling on her cheeks and flickering slightly as she dreams her mysterious dreams.

I don't know about her dreams, but I know about mine, and while I wouldn't call them wonderful, I can't ever forget them. Especially that one I get all the time. I'm staring into the far distance where I can see the towers of a city burning, burning. What does all that mean?

It's still too early for anyone to be up other than the slaves. I run into several of them as I dive down the warren

7

of corridors and curving back stairs that keep the palace operating. Some are lugging cauldrons of hot water for royal baths, some have been collecting apples or figs for royal breakfasts, some have been emptying royal chamber pots. Royal shit is just as smelly as everyone else's.

Me, I have to collect my brazier from the kitchens, but there's something else I want to do. Something secret.

I just hope he isn't there today, watching me.

I leave the dark, enclosed, musty air of the palace and go outside through the courtyard where the guard is coming to the end of his night shift and yawning. One or two guards stand on the high wall, looking over to the sea. It's been a quiet night – been a quiet few days, in fact. We have no idea what the Greeks are up to in their great city of tents and beached ships a mile away. As long as they're quiet, who cares?

That's what people here think, anyway.

Although there's a main gate well guarded to the palace, there are half a dozen secret ways in and out. I leave by a little back door where a drain used to run out beneath the walls. The drain is gone now, but the door is still there, and it's seldom locked. It leads to a narrow passage that winds down to the other building here at the high point of the citadel, where the paved road comes to an end. It's an ancient building, patched, re-patched, burned, earthquake-damaged and put together again. It's just a big, high-sided windowless hall, roofed with red tiles. In front, two steps lead to a portico with four squat pillars painted red, fading and peeling, and behind them there's a massive plain door, which is barred shut.

I've never been inside of course. Only the priestesses can do that. But there's something precious and ancient there – a statue of the goddess – Pallas, they call her here – Athene we called her in our country. The kind and wise goddess with her spear and helmet. The statue goes back into the mists of time. People who've seen it say it's small, no bigger than a man's forearm, and made of wood blackened and smoothed with age. But it's the most potent thing in the citadel, they say. If it's ever lost or taken, then Troy will surely fall. The goddess is pleased to inhabit it and attend to people's prayers.

That's why I'm coming out of the little passage and crossing the road, with my sandals slapping on the paving stones, and the dawn air cold in my throat. I try to do this every day, and my mistress never knows.

The door is shut; Athene's priestess still sleeps in her low house next door. There's a big terracotta dish on the terrace, and those who love the goddess leave what they can for her.

There's nothing there now, and I place my gift carefully. A sweet honey cake I stole from the dish I was passing to my mistress last night. I've kept it in my pocket all night and it's crumbled a bit, but I utter a fervent prayer to my special goddess as I leave it there, 'Please, Holy Athene, don't let me be a slave for the rest of my life!' Some days it's a flower, or a coin that I'm given for doing a task nicely, or a small cup of wine, or a collop of roast meat from my supper. As long as I put something there, and say my prayer, I feel sure the goddess hears me.

My mistress wouldn't like this of course. Apollo is her god: his temple is half a mile from the Scaean Gate in the middle of the plain. Dangerous to go there these days, so we take guards. We'll be going later this morning, with Madam all dressed in her finery. She goes once a week to lay offerings and send prayers.

Now I have to go back to the palace. Of course, I pause for just a moment, to enjoy this last taste of something that feels the same as freedom. I stand at the top of the hill and look down the winding road. To my right there's the wall and gate to the palace. To my left, beyond the temple and the priestesses' house, I can see the columned doorways of great houses. A dog sniffs at the gutter; someone flings open a shuttered window. I can smell baking bread in the air.

But today, and I'm grateful, I don't see *him*. I don't think he's there for me: I think it's for my mistress, but I can't be sure. It's just that every day for, what, the last several weeks, he's been there, at some point, standing in the shadows, by a wall, on a staircase, looking through a window grille.

He's young, tall and fair – that's all that I can tell for sure. Some days he's taller. Once his hair was darker. He can come and go. Walls don't seem to bother him. I see him, but I don't think my mistress does, which is odd, for all her talk of dreams and Second Sight. If I tap my mistress on the arm and ask her to look, he's gone by the time she turns. Once I passed right close to him, and he was looking at me, as my mistress ran up the stairs ahead of us. I turned and looked at him in a querying way, and I saw him give a faint half smile and a shake of his head. It was so dark on the stairs that I could scarcely make him out, just a white gleam in his eyes and the sheen of his lips. He was very handsome, but unreal, like a statue.

I don't think he's mortal. But who is he? And what is he doing?

Chapter Two

Sometimes you can almost forget that there's a war on. For weeks there's been no movement from the black ships. Almost as if everyone's gone home, though of course they haven't.

Actually the rumour is that at the moment they're too busy arguing with each other to have time to think about us.

This afternoon, everything is quiet in the citadel. Some of our men are exercising on the plain far below us, throwing javelins, shooting arrows, running races, but they're laughing and at ease as though it was just an ordinary day. As we go through the cramped little streets of the lower town, we see men who on other days might be fighting, sitting in their doorways, polishing up their swords or rubbing oil into leather breastplates. They jump to their feet and bow as my lady hurries past.

We've finished in the temple and have to hurry because we're supposed to visit the King, her father. He likes each member of his family to come to see him at least once a week. And there are a lot of family.

Through the Scaean Gate, up the curve of the paved road that runs through the upper citadel, through the palace gate, across the courtyards, through the heavy bronze and carved wood doors, across the main hall, through the family doors at the end, up the stairs, and down the long corridor where the unmarried sons sleep, to the King's room. A guard jumps to attention and flings the door open. Cassandra strides through.

It's a windy day down on the plain and the curl has already come out of Cassandra's hair; she looks dishevelled and a little red around the nose and cheeks. We didn't see him on the way back – maybe he wouldn't like her looking like this.

The private chamber of the King and Queen is one of the largest in the palace. It's built into a curve of the wall, and three large windows look out towards the sea – which must have been a fine view before the Greek armies went and camped there. The murals show sea creatures and waving sea plants in turquoise blue, starred here and there with crimson. Sometimes I feel as though I'm deep in Poseidon's kingdom, and the King, sitting tall and very straight, with his silvery hair and beard, on his chair inlaid with silver and mother-of-pearl, is Poseidon himself.

Prince Hector is there already, talking to the King. He's a big man, Hector, broad shoulders, strong arms, a loud voice. His dark hair and beard are clipped short and unfussy. He's wearing civilian clothes today, a kilt of white wool trimmed with blue. His suntanned legs are bare.

The King sits, thoughtfully. The Queen, Lady Hecuba, sits as she always does, at her loom. Today she's weaving a narrow band, incredibly intricate, of crimson, gold and deep green. One day it will edge a royal cloak.

'Cassandra, my darling, it's good to see you,' says her father, in his slow deep voice, rising from his seat to embrace her.

Hector grins and says, 'Hello, Sister.'

'Cassandra, dear,' says her mother. I stand silent and motionless behind her. Their eyes pass over and through me as though I'm transparent. Nobody notices a slave.

Hector continues what he was saying to the King. 'It's bad, apparently. Dozens already.'

'Just imagine all those funeral pyres,' says the Queen with a shudder. 'The smell!'

'What's happened?' asks Cassandra. 'What's going on?'

'Did you pay your respects to the god?' asks the King, changing the subject. Cassandra sighs, but she must answer his question first. She tells him that yes, a young goat was sacrificed by the attendant priestesses, yes, it was a good sacrifice, though the wind made it hard to get the sacrificial fire going, that she poured wine as well, and she felt that the god would have been pleased.

I didn't tell her who'd been standing in the shadows smiling at her...

'So what's going on at the Greek camp?' she asks her brother now she's got the King's questions out of the way.

'Sickness and fever,' he says with a smile. 'My man was down there this morning. Going through them like wildfire, apparently.'

'Good,' says Cassandra. 'I hope they all die. Their punishment for taking that girl.'

A few weeks ago the Greeks kidnapped a girl. Chryseis was the daughter of a powerful priest, and it's better to leave such people alone. But she'd been visiting Lyrnessus for a festival, and it was on that day that the Greeks decided to overrun the town and take what they wanted from it. Agamemnon had at once decided Chryseis was to be his prize, poor girl. He even went round saying that he preferred her to his wife Clytemnestra – which will go down well if ever that news gets back home.

We know all this because Hector has a spy in the Greek camp. He passes as a Greek and spends his days there listening and being careful. Then he comes and tells Hector what's going on.

My people, the Greeks. No, I don't want them to die. But I don't want this city to be the loser in a war. I can't imagine what would happen to us all, to me, to the Queen, to my mistress...I'm a slave now, but as slaves go, I'm lucky. If they lose the war, I won't be lucky.

'I don't think you should wish even your worst enemy a death from fever,' says her mother reprovingly.

'Oh, I don't know,' says the King. 'The more we get rid of now, the fewer of them to come making nuisances of themselves. Yes, let's hope Apollo, blessed be his name, kills them all off. Now, Hector, are you going to bring in my dear little grandson for a visit? I haven't seen him for far too long.'

In a room just down the corridor, combing her lovely hair, or making delicate tapestries, is the reason why they're all here, the Lady Helen.

There's a story – there's always a story – that it was the goddess Aphrodite herself who had singled out Lady Helen to be Paris's bride. In those days, Paris, one of the King's younger sons, spent much of his time out on the plain, tending his flocks. Too many princes rubbing about in the palace in peacetime makes for irritations and quarrels. But then one day, as he was sitting on a hillside, three goddesses appeared in front of him – just like that. Most of us never get to see one – but here was Paris – he is very handsome, I'll grant that – getting three at once; Hera, Aphrodite and Artemis. They'd been having some sort of a competition – over a golden apple, inscribed 'For the Fairest'. And that had put the cat among the pigeons, because it had to go to one of them; goddesses are all beautiful – why would you want to be a goddess if you couldn't be beautiful? And they couldn't decide – so they asked Paris. That's the story the poets have already started telling. And it suits Paris, so he doesn't contradict them.

Anyway, Paris chose Aphrodite, partly because she was gorgeous, partly because she'd promised him the most beautiful earthly woman for himself.

Well, no doubt who the most beautiful earthly woman was – we'd even heard of her on our little island – we used to sing songs about her. It was Helen of Sparta, daughter, so they say, of Zeus. And already married to King Menelaus.

So what does Paris do, but jump into a boat, go over there, and carry her off? She didn't go unwillingly; they fell head-over-heels in love with each other. She left her husband behind, and also her daughter who was a few years younger than me when all this happened.

Sometimes, Lady Helen borrows me from Cassandra and talks to me. I think she's lonely here. Apart from one old woman, all her slaves are Trojan.

I speak Greek, and so does Lady Helen. Sometimes we talk about home, the high mountains, the rocky shores, the scent of thyme on the air. I can hardly remember my Greek island. But talking to the Lady Helen brings it all back.

Yes, she's beautiful. I can well believe she's the most beautiful woman in the world. But she's also lonely. And I think at the moment that's the main thing about her.

Chapter Three

This is the second summer that the Greeks have been camped here, gathered in the harbour, just out of sight. If you stand on the ramparts you can make out the dirty haze of their smoke, and if the wind's in the right direction, you can hear them shouting or singing.

I don't think either side thought it was going to take so long. First Agamemnon's navy did a bit of looting and burning along the coast, for no particular reason – that's why the Trojans think they're just pirates. Then they got lost, far south at Mysia, where they got entangled with the armies of King Telephos, and spent the whole winter there, fighting and looting. Then the following spring, sailed north again, and this time Troy wasn't so lucky.

Still, they'd been a long time coming, and that had given King Priam a chance to prepare. He'd called allies from all over the plain, and they'd all sent men, as they hate the Greeks. The plain to the north of the city, which used to be so peaceful, just the horse-breeding fields and the blue acres of flax, is now full of army camps, tents and huts and hastily thrown up defences. If the Greeks have thousands of men, so do the Trojans.

When the Greeks landed here, I think both sides thought they'd have an easy victory. I remember the day well, how the Trojans and their allies set off for the beach as soon as the watchmen had reported the black ships on the horizon. The day was bright and clear, and thousands of bronze spears flashed in the sun and they chanted songs of triumph. They'd massed spears and chariots against the invaders but the Greeks fought back, even though they were just stumbling out of their ships on to shore.

That was an evening of funeral pyres and weeping women, of men with horrible wounds, and the dusty survivors limping back to the city, no longer singing.

Then there was a long period in which both sides recouped their powers and waited. The Trojans struck next, a great battle down by the beach, but still they couldn't drive the Greeks away. It's been like that ever since, sometimes great clashing battles, sometimes sneaky groups of men at night trying to burn each other's supplies or catch sleeping men out. But the cost of all those men plundering our resources has been huge – many small farms have been burned and cattle and horses stolen, many farmers have fled to the interior. Nearly all the horse-breeders have gone inland; only Hector's great stud remains out in the plain, guarded all the time. He had a famous way with horses, before the war, but I don't think he's had much time for them lately.

This is how it is – sometimes the war, but like now, long periods of eerie peace. I'm no war commander but it would seem to me that if the Greeks are laid low with illness, now would be a good time to attack them. But King Priam doesn't see things this way. He thinks the Greeks will get fed up and go home. I'm not so sure. At the centre of all this is Lady Helen's abandoned husband, Menelaus; it was his anger and hurt pride that fuelled this expedition in the first place. He must want revenge on Paris for stealing his wife, revenge on Lady Helen for leaving him. By all accounts, Menelaus is a tough, angry fighter; he won't settle for any compromises.

And of course he is brother to the High King of the Greeks, Agamemnon. Agamemnon will support his brother. And he has an agenda of his own – by all accounts, he's always short of gold to pay his allies, and is always on the lookout for an excuse to plunder more lands to satisfy his greed for gold.

Troy has – or at least it had, before all this started – huge reserves of gold, hidden away in stone-lined storerooms deep in the palace cellars. The Greeks won't be happy till they get their hands on it.

Prince Hector doesn't agree with his father's policy of inaction. He urges him to take the initiative, harass the Greeks while they're weak. But the King insists this is the best way. 'Why waste Trojan blood when nature will kill them for us?'

'They'll recover from this plague, and then they'll come back, worse than ever. You know that, Father.'

'I know nothing of the sort. I know that my sons and my people live, and they might not do if they went down to the harbour and attacked the Greeks. Besides, they'll run out of food soon. They'll sail home before the winter, tails between their legs is my guess.'

But they aren't running out of food. In fact they seem to have plenty of it. When they run short here they simply send ships across the Straits to their own lands, and return laden with supplies. If the Trojans had ships, they could go after them and take them on at sea. But the Trojans don't, not war ships anyway, and all their fishing fleet will have been taken by the Greeks by now. It's another of those things that Hector and his father argue about. Hector's been urging his father for years to build up a navy, but the King refuses. Navies are for pirates, and the Trojans aren't pirates.

So the stalemate continues. It isn't war and it isn't peace. No one's winning. No one's losing.

And Hector and his father are going to have an argument soon. Hector clenches and unclenches his fists. Then he remembers something to change the mood. 'Let me send for the boy, Father,' he says. He knows Priam adores his grandson – Hector is a special son and Astyanax a very special grandson.

Hector looks round the room and sees me. 'Fetch him, Eirene,' he says. 'If that's all right with you, of course.' This last comment is addressed to Cassandra, not me.

I go off obediently, through the heavy doors, and down the Corridor of the Sons, the shining pillared corridor off which Priam's sons by Hecuba live. There are other sons, of course, Priam had many concubines when he was younger – but these mostly live below the palace in the mansions in the citadel. There's less room but more prestige for the sons who live here.

Andromache and Hector share the grandest room – apart from the King's. There is a great carved wooden bed, and tapestries on the wall, a hunting scene against emerald green spattered with tiny flowers.

Andromache is sitting on a stool, gazing into a bronze mirror, frowning slightly, as though she doesn't like what she sees. She's looking tired and drawn, certainly – the strain of this war is telling on her more than most. But she's tall and queenly, with her aristocratic little hawk's nose and her thoughtful grey eyes. A couple of attendants are in the room with her, their spindles twisting silently. The baby is asleep in his high wooden cot with ivory tigers and jaguars running around it.

I pass on Hector's request. She doesn't look best pleased. 'I've only just got him down,' she says with a sigh. 'Still, Father must be obeyed.'

She turns and calls for the nursemaid, but the nursemaid's not there. 'She had a bad stomach, Madam,' says one of the maids.

Andromache pulls a face. 'Then you'll have to take him,' she says to me. She sees the look on my face. 'What's the matter? Never held a baby before?'

Oh, yes I have; there was my little sister Larisa, with her dribbly smile and soft little hands always tugging at my curls.

'Wake him up slowly, so he doesn't cry. Think you can do that?'

'Yes, Madam.'

'*She* isn't there, I hope.' *She* is Lady Helen, who Andromache doesn't care to bump in to, any more than she has to.

'No, Madam.'

I pick up the baby. He is soft and smells of new bread. He doesn't wake up, but his head, with its silky dark hair, lolls against my shoulder...

And a few moments later the High King of Troy is on his hands and knees crawling round the floor after a giggling baby.

Chapter Four

Some time later, Cassandra and I go back to her room. She's been wearing her priestess robes all morning and they've heavy. She looks tired and a little bedraggled. She kicks off her dusty sandals, which have marked her feet with red stripes. I help her out of the embroidered skirt and bodice, and slip a simple linen robe over her head. She sighs with relief and rubs her waist where the skirt band has dug into it. 'Phew! That's better. Now let's get all this stuff off my hair.'

She throws herself on to the bed, and relieved, I take the comb and sit down next to her. I've been standing around all morning, out in the dust of the plain and in the palace, and I'm tired too.

I lift the diadem off her head and lay it carefully down, then I pick up a hank of her fair hair and start to comb it slowly. We're neither of us in any hurry to finish – it's just good to be sitting here in the quiet. And sometimes, when we're on our own like this, she seems to forget that I'm her slave, and she talks to me as she'd talk to another human being. I like her when she's in this mood – though I have to be careful not to step out of line, as she can snap in a minute. It's a bit lonely for her, I suppose. Priam has other daughters, but not by Hecuba; they live in the lower town and they're a bit disdainful of her and the airs she gives herself. Really, she has no companion of her own age to talk to, so in moments like this, I'll do.

'That poor girl!' she says. 'I can't stop thinking of her.' Yes, she's been obsessed with Chryseis, Agamemnon's captive, though she's never met her. She's been talking about her ever since we heard the news. 'She was only visiting Lyrnessus when those Greeks came! Imagine just being carted away like old rubbish.'

'Yes, Madam,' I say, grimly. 'I can certainly imagine that.'

'Oh. Yes, I'd forgotten about you. But at least you were lucky.'

'Was I, Madam?'

'You ended up here with us. Poor Chryseis ended up with Agamemnon, the man who sacrificed his own daughter, the monster. How could any father do that? What was your father at home by the way, a carpenter?'

'A boat-builder, Madam.'

'Oh. But even so. You'd never have got to live like this in your dirty little village. Look at you, wearing clothes a princess wore! And you never ever go hungry!'

Well, that's certainly true. The robe I'm wearing – pale pink embroidered linen and only a few darns in it – is one of Madam's cast-offs. She's taller than me, so I'm usually there to fit into her last year's dresses. And yes, there's far more food than I can ever eat.

But there's also the little matter of something called freedom. I think she might consider that.

Of course she's not going to waste any of her precious princess-time thinking about my liberty. I know that, and as I slowly and gently comb out the dust and tangles from her hair, I don't really mind, just for the moment. Yes, I could be worse off. But I could be better off, too.

Then she says something that makes me startle, and I don't know why. 'I just keep thinking of her, like that. A priest's daughter, and a priestess herself. And now she has to be groped by some filthy old man!'

As she says that, I suddenly catch a tangle in her hair and can't stop myself tugging the comb through it sharply. She screams and sits up, hand raised as if she's going to hit me.

Then she sees my face.

'Eirene, what is it?'

I try to look normal again. 'Nothing, Madam. I'm sorry, Madam.'

For I can't tell her what I saw. For a moment, I had a picture in my mind, which I saw as clearly as I can now see her startled face. A big man, dark-haired, middle-aged, smiling a nasty smile. And he's got a girl under his big hands, whom he's clutching as a cat clutches a mouse. The girl's face is full of terror and loathing. It's not Chryseis, whom I've never met. It's Cassandra.

'You're trembling,' she says, quite gently. 'Are you all right?'

'I'm all right,' I say, composing myself. 'I...I was just remembering my...mother.' I often think of my mother, but I wasn't just then. But it's a convenient lie.

She pats my hand. 'I'm sorry, Eirene. But remember, we're your family now. The royal House of Troy is your family.'

'Yes, thank you. I'm grateful, Madam.' I'm not, but

that doesn't matter. The main thing is not to let her know what I saw.

More and more, I get these little snatches of things I haven't yet seen. I don't know what it means.

Cassandra forgets me and my supposed homesickness in a moment, and is off again. 'And her father even came looking for her. That was so brave of him. Only to get insulted by that pig Agamemnon. I wonder if my father would come looking for me if I were captured.'

'His Majesty would do anything for his children,' I say. 'I'm sure of that.' This isn't a lie, at least. I think he would.

'But I won't be captured. My brother Hector will see to that. I know we'll be victorious.'

Well, the Trojans may have Hector. But the Greeks have got Achilles; as great a champion, if not greater. But I don't say this. I say, 'Everyone says Troy can't be taken. Not while the statue of Pallas Athene stays in her temple.'

'Exactly,' she says. 'And just look at our walls. I bet they don't have such walls in your country. Eirene, be careful! What's got into you this morning? You're hurting me again.'

'I'm sorry, Madam,' I say.

Another strange thing happens this evening. I'm walking on the ramparts with my mistress, and we reach the part where you can look down through the walls into the winding streets of the upper town. A noise draws our attention. A group of boys – I don't know who they are; slaves from the lower town, I think, are gathering in front of a house. One of them picks up a stone and throws it. Then another. There's much laughter.

Then I see what they're throwing stones at. A little owl sits huddled on the window sill. It doesn't fly away, so it must be hurt.

Cassandra sees them and shrugs. 'Nasty boys,' she says, and turns away.

But I can't turn away. 'Excuse me, Madam,' I say.

We're not far from the stairs that coil down into the city. I run down them as fast as I can, through the palace gate, into the courtyard, and out into the city. The boys are still there, halfway down a street of small houses where palace officials live. I dive into their midst, using elbows, shoulders, knees, anything I can do to shove.

They're big boys, six or so of them, greasy and sweaty. They laugh and make obscene noises as I ram into them. But I'm so angry, I won't stop. 'What in Hades do you think you're doing, you brutes?'

One of them is in the act of picking up a stone. He pauses for a moment, long enough for me to look at the owl, hunched in its ground floor window.

Their mocking catcalls surround me, but I don't hear them. I'm vaguely aware that Cassandra is leaning over the parapet, also shouting something. One of them sees her, and nudges the others. They slink away down the hill towards the lower town.

The owl is still there, big topaz eyes unblinking in its round face. I have to climb up on to a flower pot to reach it, but I do. It's surprisingly light. It digs its sharp talons into my arm. I try to settle it in the crook of my arm so it can't bite or scratch, and amazingly it stays still. I can't tell if it's been injured.

I go back upstairs, carefully now, clutching my little

bundle. I can feel its tiny heart beating under the feathers. My mistress is appalled.

'Whatever have you got there?'

'They were throwing stones at it,' I say.

'Yes, I saw that. I can't bear cruel boys. But why have you brought it up here?'

'It'll die if I don't.'

'You aren't going to look after it, are you?'

'It can go in my room.'

'It'll poo everywhere.'

'I'll clean it up.'

'But you can't...Why don't you just leave it?'

'I can't do that, Madam. What would the goddess say?'

That gets through to her. Owls are sacred to my goddess, and Cassandra knows that, even though her goddess is Artemis, not Athene. She turns away from me.

'Well, do what you have to. Only don't come to me covered in owl-poo, all right?'

'Thank you, Madam.'

'It'll probably die, anyway.'

But it doesn't die. I take it into my little room, and I make a nest from a pile of rags for it in a corner of the floor. I make sure the window is open so it can fly out if it wants to. I put a bowl of water in front of it, and then work out how I'm going to get dead mice.

This isn't the first time I've rescued an owl. My brothers found one once, and we kept it in the woodshed for a few days. I learned how to feed it, and we tried to look after it. But sadly it died. I think it had broken its wing.

I don't try to examine this little one, to see if it's broken anything. I wouldn't know what to look for. All

I can hope to do is to keep it safely in my room while it decides whether or not it's going to get better or to die. It looks at me with its huge yellow eyes, moving its head from side to side. 'I'll do my best,' I say to it.

I go down into the kitchen. Iso, the kitchen boy, is one of my friends, but even he looks askance when I ask him about dead mice. 'You're joking!' he says.

By this time some of the other slaves have gathered around us. Some of them, like me, have a special feeling for Athene, and they're surprisingly anxious to help me save her sacred bird. There are mice in one of the cellars. Usually they let the cat loose on them, but someone says they'll make a trap and leave it there tonight instead.

Which they do, and in the morning I go downstairs to find three squealing mice.

I hadn't thought in advance about the next bit. It isn't pleasant. I have to kill the tiny wriggling things, chop them into bits and take them up to feed my new pet.

The little owl seems brighter this morning, though she still hasn't moved. She gobbles up the furry mouthfuls and continues to stare at me. I can hardly bring myself to think about what I've done to get them to her.

All this before my mistress is awake. I scrub my hands to get rid of the smells of mouse and owl, and then I go to attend to her. From time to time, I peep into my room, hoping the little thing will have flown away to safety, but she's still there. Almost as though she wants to be here.

She stays for three days. For three nights, I lie down to sleep on my mattress next to her. She doesn't utter a sound all night. On the morning of the fourth day, she's gone.

Chapter Five

We're sitting in Queen Hecuba's room at our looms when one of Lady Helen's slaves comes in. She comes over to me. 'My lady wishes to see you,' she says in my ear. I look up, anxiously. Andromache isn't here, which is good, or she'd have something to say about the Lady Helen giving orders. I don't know what Queen Hecuba feels about the Lady Helen, but she doesn't complain when I go over and ask her. 'Go on, then,' she says with a shrug.

Lady Helen doesn't sit with the others at their looms. Andromache would be sure to try and pick a quarrel with her, and I think Lady Helen likes to feel she's above such things. My mistress isn't here either, luckily. She's having a music lesson downstairs. Slaves don't need to know music. But it means I don't have to explain to her.

I know what Lady Helen wants me to do. I've done it for her several times before.

Before I get to her room, I see the King's son, Paris, coming out of the door. He's looking very jaunty, his long hair hanging down his back, his tunic swinging. He's very handsome, the Lord Paris, with big brown long-lashed eyes and a nice smile. Still, I slither past him with my back to the wall. He has a reputation among the slave girls. I don't think he does anything more than pinch, though; with the most beautiful woman in the world as his new wife, he doesn't need to.

He flashes me a saucy smile though. 'Ah, it's the beautiful Eirene! How's the toothache?' For he remembers things, does Paris, my name, and that the last time he saw me, I had a bad tooth.

'Better now, thank you, sir.'

'Good. We can't have our little Eirene in pain, can we? Have you come to see my lovely wife?'

'If you please, sir.'

'Good. Well, see if you can improve her mood today. She's missing those Spartan plains, I think. I can't say anything right.'

And he tosses his long hair over his shoulder and goes off whistling a tune. He doesn't seem too unhappy that Lady Helen's in a mood.

I push open the door and go inside.

Lady Helen sits with her back to me. She's holding a distaff and spindle in her hands, but she isn't spinning. From the angle of her head, I'd say she was looking far into distances none of the rest of us can see.

I love going into her room. Rich red and gold tapestries hang on the wall, and candles glow in brass lanterns studded with holes, so that the light glimmers and sparks. There are chests of carved and gilded wood, and cushions of that wonderful shimmering fabric that comes from far away India. There's a heavy sweet scent in the air, roses or jasmine, and she has fresh flowers brought in from the plain nearly every day.

In the corner, her old slave-woman Aethra sleeps, snoring gently. There are no other women present.

Lady Helen hears the sound of the door closing, and

turns to see me. She's wearing her hair loose today and it cascades like a waterfall over her shoulder as she turns her head. It's a rich deep brown with threads of gold in it that catch all the light from the candles.

'Eirene, is that you?' she says in her soft and husky voice.

I go and stand before her. She smiles up at me.

I'm not sure that I like the Lady Helen entirely, and I can't approve of everything she does. I know I shan't be easy with the task she's about to give me, for instance. But it's impossible not to be stunned by her beauty, every time you see her; those perfect features, that skin like flower petals, those eyes with so many colours in their depths, green, hazel, gold, framed by long lashes. She's sitting now, but you can see the graceful lines of her arms and wrists, her long neck, and you can tell that when she stands up, she'll be more beautiful than any statue.

'Eirene, darling,' she says. 'How are you today?'

'Well, thank you, my lady.'

She sighs. 'Of course, you have no reason not to be, have you?'

Well, not if you don't count being a slave, I suppose. But I don't say anything.

'I just felt like talking in my own language for once,' she says. Most of the Trojans speak a bit of Greek, but with such a harsh accent, you don't like to hear it. I know she wants to talk, but that isn't all she wants.

'I was remembering the anemones on the hill slopes,' she goes on. 'Did you have anemones near you?'

When I was little, flowers were flowers. White ones, pink ones or yellow ones. They didn't have names then, though I've learned a little about flowers since. 'I think so, Madam.'

She sighs. 'The flowers here are so brash – where they grow at all.' She points towards the big white scentless daisies in a jar on the windowsill. 'I shall have to give up my flowers soon, I fear. My man has to go farther and farther away to find them for me. I can't go on asking him.'

'I'm sorry, Madam.'

'How old are you, Eirene?'

'Me, Madam?' I say, foolishly, for there's no one else about apart from the sleeping old woman. 'About fourteen…I think.'

'My daughter will be almost sixteen by now. When I went away she was only eleven. I often wonder what she's like now, whether she remembers me.'

'I'm sure she does, Madam.'

'I hear that she's married now – I can't imagine that – my little girl. And do you know who she's married to?'

'No, Madam.'

'To the son of Achilles, who's now out to kill us all. Just like her father, she's lined up against me…I'm sure she hates me for what I did…I keep thinking of her, making daisy chains in the meadow, her little mouth set. Such a determined little thing. And that red hair of her father's, like deep copper. But there, too late for regrets now. I've been sleeping badly recently, Eirene. That's why I'm talking so foolishly. What's done is done…'

She must see disapproval on my face, for she looks up at me with a melting smile. 'I couldn't help it, child. Love, like a tidal wave. It was quite overwhelming when it came. You'll understand some day.'

31

Will I? I'm not sure that I ever will. Loving someone to the exclusion of all reason doesn't seem right to me. When I fantasize sometimes about my future, I don't see myself hanging on to some man. Instead, I have a picture in my mind of a little garden, high on a hill, where I grow myrtles and hyacinths, and keep a few little hens, and perhaps a cat for company. It's such a vivid picture, almost like one of my strange sudden images. It's not a man I want to serve; I want to serve my goddess.

But of course I have no chance of serving anyone until I die, apart from my Lady Cassandra and whoever she will pass me on to one day. The family of Troy! Some family, when you're a slave.

And my job now is to fetch what Lady Helen wants me to fetch. She opens a little purse at her belt and slips me a couple of coins. '*Will* you, darling? And remember...' She puts her finger to her lips. Sssh. Don't tell anyone, not Paris, not the king. And certainly not the old lady in the corner who's been with her for years and would be angry if she found out.

I leave the palace and the upper town. Through the Scaean Gate and into the jumble and confusion of the lower town, full of animal and cooking smells, of dirty gutters, of all the things being sold in the dozens of little shops with their open fronts. Here the smell of leather, here spices, here cheap perfume. You'd never think with all this stuff on show that there was a war on.

But what I want is a tiny alleyway, tucked between a butchers and a wine shop, down narrow stairs, slippery with slops and garbage. There's a dark doorway, a dried branch of herbs nailed to the side, a leather curtain hung over it.

I push the curtain aside and go in. He's there, hunched over his little counter, a little dark man, pouring stuff into tiny pottery vials. The air is thick and heavy. There's almost no light. I don't know how he sees.

'Oh, it's you again,' he says, and he says it in Greek. Proper Greek, not Trojan Greek. I know his name is Myron, and that he's to be found at the Branch of Hyssop. I don't imagine he knows my name.

I put the coins on the table. He reaches into a little cupboard and brings out a tiny flask of blue glass. 'This is what you want, I think.' No explanations; he knows better than that.

And I thrust the little vial into my skirt and make my way back up the narrow steps and through the town, taking to my Lady Helen the stuff that will make her forget her loneliness and her homesickness, and bring her sleep as black as death.

Chapter Six

It's early the next morning. My mistress has woken up and
banged on the partition between our rooms with the stick
she keeps for the purpose. Blearily I stumble into her room.
I'm not properly awake, and the dreams I've been having –
dreams in which I'm walking over rocky mountain slopes,
studded with anemones, free as a bird – are still chasing
through my head, still more real, before they start to fade,
than my mistress and her demands.

My mistress has used her chamber pot, and she
doesn't want it in the room with her, so I must empty it.
The latrines are on a bend of the corridor, just by the main
stairs. Still half asleep, I clutch the pot and stumble into
the corridor.

I haven't seen him for some time. He's standing with
his back to the wall, just where he can see the door to
my mistress's room. The corridor is gloomy, and the early
morning light comes through with pearly opalescence.
There is a faint glow about him, as though he's carrying
a lamp, but he's holding nothing. The crown of golden
hair, the face like a beautiful mask, eyes like sloes. No
expression. He wears a silvery tunic, silver greaves, a belt
clasped with dull jewels. I know who he is.

I've never confronted him head-on like this before.
And I'm struck with embarrassment that I'm meeting a god

while carrying a pot of piss. I can't walk past him today. I put the pot down on the floor, and stand up slowly. He considers me, head on one side, and the faintest of smiles curving his mouth.

How do you talk to a god? 'What do you want from me?' I say. And add, 'My Lord.'

He's silent for a long while, still considering me. His face gleams in the darkness. Then he speaks, his voice low and a little hollow.

'It's not you I want, girl. You're spoken for.'

'What…what do you mean?'

'Never mind. You'll find out. But tell your mistress to be ready for me. One day soon.'

I'm confused. 'Sir, I…'

'When the time comes,' he says with a cold smile, 'tell her to be ready.'

'But I don't know what you mean, my Lord.'

'Oh, I think you do,' he says, the slow smile widening. 'I think you do. Now go and do your task.'

But as I bend down to pick up the pot again, he says, 'Just ask yourself why is it that you can see me and she can't?'

I don't know what to make of this. When I come back from the latrines, he isn't there any more, for which I'm grateful. But I'm still confused and anxious. What am I supposed to say to my mistress? The gods' intentions towards us are rarely kind.

In the end, I tell her nothing. We spend a quiet day. I spin wool in the Queen's chamber. It rains all day, a grey constant drizzle that towards the evening turns stormy.

But this evening, there's an excitement that almost

puts this strange encounter out of my mind.

It's the end of the day. The big hearth fire has been put out, the tables have been cleared away, the musicians have gone to their beds. Guards hurry around, shuttering windows and bolting doors. Her room lit by a small lamp, my mistress sits on her bed, while I comb her hair and start putting it into the dozens of tiny plaits she wears at night. Outside, we can hear the rain pattering on tiles and cobbles, gurgling through the guttering. We don't either of us say very much, but I think we quite enjoy this time together, a quiet moment in the day, while we each go over its events in our own way.

I'm thinking about the god, of course, when there's a tap on the door.

It's Helenus, one of Priam's quieter and more thoughtful sons. He's also a priest of Apollo, and it's rumoured that he has the Sight. He's tall and dark, like Hector, but without the muscular shoulders and the deep resonant voice.

'You might like to hear this, you two,' he says. He has the courtesy to include me, which I like. 'Straton is here.'

Yes. Now this is interesting. Straton is one of the spies the King keeps in the Greek camp. He can't get away that often without attracting suspicion; but when he does come, it's usually worth hearing.

Cassandra jumps to her feet, her hair half plaited, and throws a robe over her shoulders. 'Come on, Eirene,' she says. I'm half amused that she's so used to me that she too includes me. I could be a Greek spy – I suppose there must be Greek spies in Troy just as there are Trojan ones in the Greek camp. I wonder who they are.

Of course, I'm not one. I couldn't spy, I don't think, no matter how much I hated my masters. I couldn't live a double life.

We make our way to Priam's great chamber. Hector is there, and Andromache, and Priam's other sons. There's Deiphobus, not quite as tall, and not quite as handsome as Hector. There's a guarded look about his eyes that makes me uncomfortable. Then there's Antiphus, and the two youngest sons, Troilus and Polites. Troilus is fair, like my mistress, and like the King was before his hair turned white. Polites and Antiphus are dark like their mother.

When we were all children, my mistress and Troilus and Polites and I would often go down to the seashore, taking a ball. The sea was less than a mile away, and as we ran over the plain, we were hardly aware of the distance. Sea-pinks and chicory flowers grew in the sandy dry ground near the sea, the wind blew strongly, and whipped up a sea far greyer and colder than the one I'd seen from my island. In the distance, the little fishing village would be going about its business, boats hauled up on to the sand, women gutting fish into leather buckets, calling and singing, men mending ropes or sails. We never minded the wind or the cold, and though I was only a slave, I was still an extra pair of hands and feet, and would be roped into the game, even though I realised early on that I was never going to be allowed to win or even do well. I enjoyed those afternoons – I could come close to being a normal child again just for a few hours. But since the Greeks arrived, the only time we've left the citadel is to go to the Temple of Apollo in the grove across the Scamander. Troilus and Polites don't have time for children's games any more.

Paris is here, in his father's chamber, but not Lady Helen. Nobody thinks that Lady Helen wants to hear too many stories about the Greeks, and about her vengeful husband Menelaus. Apart from the children of Priam and Hecuba, there are just two other special allies here, Aeneas of the Dardanians, short, stocky, with a bull neck and piercing light blue eyes, and Sarpedon, with his special friend Glaucus. Sarpedon, tall, dark and elegant, is rumoured to be a son of Zeus himself. At any rate, these three are important men, so it's not surprising they're there to hear the spy tell his story.

Straton, the spy, is sitting shivering on a pile of furs in the midst of every one. Someone has taken his soaking cloak from him, and thrown a sheepskin over him. He's cradling hot wine in his hands. But soon he's ready to tell his news.

And it's important news. Something very significant has happened in the Greek camp.

Chapter Seven

The Greek camp is divided into two. The largest part, where the old fishing village used to stand, is a city of tents surrounded by hastily dug ditches and palisades; it is where Agamemnon, Menelaus and most of their allies are camped. Their black ships are drawn up upon the shore, rank upon rank of them.

But beyond them, and separate from them, as he always is, is Achilles. His men are called Myrmidons and they're loyal only to him. There are fewer of them, and their tented city is altogether cleaner and neater, while Achilles himself is housed in a fine palatial building, made of wood and earth, roofed with thorn bushes, and hung with tapestries. With him are his dear friend Patroclus, without whom he goes nowhere, and a girl called Briseis. Like Chryseis, Briseis is also a war captive, but unlike that old letch Agamemnon, Achilles adores her and treats her with all the dignity of a queen.

This much we all know. But we didn't know what happened the other day.

There's been a good deal of discontent in the Greek camp because of the sickness and fever. People don't want to say it out loud, but they're blaming Agamemnon, because he not only captured a girl who was performing service to Apollo in Lyrnessus where she was taken, but he also insulted her father, a priest of Apollo. Apollo is angry, they say; hence the plague.

There's a priest called Calchas. Agamemnon dislikes him because he told the King to sacrifice his own daughter at Aulis to get a favourable wind for the fleet. Agamemnon reluctantly obeyed, and they got their wind. The goddess Artemis had been angry with him then. Now it's Apollo, Artemis's twin. There seems to be something of a pattern here.

If the visitor in the corridor was who I think it was, and if the look in his cold dark eyes is only a small part of his anger, then I wouldn't like to bring down his full anger upon myself.

Anyway, this time Calchas's advice to the King was simpler, and didn't involve sacrificing anybody. He must send back Chryseis to her father.

On hearing this, apparently, Agamemnon went into an almighty sulk. He loved Chryseis, she was his property, he certainly wasn't going to give her back. She was going to live with him in Mycenae forever, working at her loom, warming his bed, until she grew old and grey.

The Greek leaders met in Agamemnon's tent and went over and over the problem. Chryseis must go back, or the plague would get them all. But Agamemnon's pride would be badly dented if she did. And that too would be dangerous for the Greeks.

Then Agamemnon came up with a solution that would save his own face at least. A nasty, selfish solution that would please no one else.

Yes, he'd send Chryseis back. But in return he wanted the girl whom Achilles had taken, Briseis.

At once there was uproar. Achilles leapt to his feet, eyes blazing. He called Agamemnon names that no one except he would dare use in addressing the High King. Briseis was his – he'd won her fairly, and anyway Agamemnon always took the lion's share of the spoils. Achilles owed him nothing.

I don't suppose he said, in front of all the men, that he loved the girl. But I think he did, in his own way.

And of course, in all this, no one asked Briseis what her feelings were. She was just a girl.

The argument continued. At one point it even seemed that Achilles would take out his sword and plunge it into Agamemnon's heart – which would have solved a lot of problems for the Trojans. But he didn't, in the end. He held back the worst of his anger, and stormed back to his tent, Patroclus, his beloved friend, laying a soothing hand on his shoulder. But even Patroclus couldn't soothe Achilles.

Worse was to follow. The next day, Agamemnon sent two of his men to take Briseis, by force, if necessary. In the end, even Achilles had to obey the High King. He let them take the girl. Reluctantly, she trailed behind the men, casting mournful glances behind her, as though she hoped that Achilles would come to her rescue. But he didn't. He went down to the shore, the great hero, put his head in his arms and wept bitterly.

That evening, he decided he was going to take his ships and his men back to Phthia. He had no real grudge against the Trojans, after all. He was only there because long ago, Patroclus had been one of Lady Helen's suitors, and all the unsuccessful ones had taken an oath that if Lady Helen was ever in danger, they would rescue her. I'm not

41

sure that Lady Helen's current position counts as danger, at least as far as she's concerned, but anyway they'd taken their oath and here they were. And where Patroclus went, there went Achilles, so devoted were they.

But if Achilles and all his men, who were the finest fighters in the Greek lands went back home, then the rest of the Greeks would be in trouble. And Calchas, the seer, who has been right about things so far, had said long ago that the Greeks could not win this war without Achilles.

King Priam was delighted. 'You see?' he said gleefully. 'What did I say? Just leave them alone, and they'll defeat themselves without our even trying.'

'They aren't defeated yet, Father,' said Hector, more soberly.

Heroes. Achilles and Hector, the men whom everyone says are the greatest heroes in the world, and now here they are, just a mile or so away from each other, though up to this moment, they have never met. Hector, who looks like a god, the son of humans, and Achilles, who looks like a man, the son of a goddess. Neither is a king now, but if they live, each will be one, one day, Hector of Troy, Achilles of Phthia.

We know something of what Achilles is like, because, although they aren't supposed to, there are still people who pass between the Greek camp and Troy, peddlers, entertainers, Phoenician traders, quack doctors, whores; not to mention spies in both directions. We learn from them that of the two men, Hector is the taller, and probably the more handsome. Achilles is shorter, stocky, broad-shouldered. He has dark blonde curls, gilded by the sun, tanned skin, and an extraordinary pair of emerald green eyes, a gift presumably from the sea-goddess who is his mother. His dearest friend is Patroclus, who was brought up with him. Achilles has a son too, like Hector, though Achilles was never married to the mother of his son. His son is called Pyrrhus, and at the moment still lives on the mainland, as Achilles feels he's still a few years too young to fight in a man's war.

He's restless and impatient, Achilles, though mostly courteous, especially to women. But his rages, when they come, are extra-human. And any man whom he chooses to fight will die. Except maybe Hector, who can match him. But no one will know this until these two come together in combat, which will probably happen one day.

There's a story that Achilles's divine mother dipped her son into a magic river to make him invulnerable, all except the heel by which she held him. I don't know if it's xtrue, but it's made everyone pretty scared of him. Which I suppose is the point of telling the story.

Hector is kind, brave, courteous (though not of course to the likes of me – Paris is courteous to me, but that's another story). He adores his wife, he adores his son. He behaves as a perfect son should to his father and mother. He's a great horseman – probably in that he outstrips Achilles; everyone says that Patroclus is better at handling horses than Achilles.

And yet, in the end, when they talk about heroes, what they're talking about is killing. What both Hector and Achilles do best is kill.

Chapter Eight

I dreamed about my home last night. I used to dream about it a lot, but now I very rarely do. The dreams used to make me sad, but now I'm pleased to have them, even though waking up to my enslavement is hard. My mother is kneeling before her quern, grinding barley, and she looks up at me reproachfully. 'Oh Eirene,' she says 'So you've decided to come back.' My brothers and sisters are there too, but they pass in a sort of blur, though they don't blur in my mind during the day; I can remember them all; my brothers Alexis, Damon and Pyros, my sister Aglaia. Yet the only one to appear distinctly in my dream is Larisa, though in the dream, she's as tall as me, but all she'll say is, 'I don't remember you,' which makes me upset.

I was the youngest for what seemed like forever, until Larisa came along, and everyone petted her instead. I remember I was a bit put out at first, until Larisa started to smile and gurgle. She seemed to particularly like being held by me; everyone said I was her special favourite. I expect the dream is right – if I saw her again, she wouldn't remember me.

And I'm sure at first that my mother would speak crossly to me; that was her way. But I know that my mother would have done anything for us. Once she took on a gang of bigger boys who'd been beating up Damon

– I can still see her, tiny and vivid, clenching her fists and looking up into their faces, and shouting at them till they were ashamed and slunk away.

I remember my father, dark, big and bearded, hammering away in his shed, working away with planks and nails and twine and pitch. He worked with my uncle, and about the time I was taken away, my oldest brother Alexis, had just started to work with him. The men in our family have built boats for as long as anyone can remember.

But most of all, I can remember the smells and sounds of our little cottage, yellowed, kite-shaped pieces of dried fish hanging from the rafters with bundles of herbs; the smoke from the central hearth that was driven back into the room on windy days and made you cough, the rough goat-skin blankets, the sound of the grindstone or the rattle of the loom, the warm, salty, dirty smell of everything, the bent thorn bush outside, on which my mother dried washing, the cloud-filled sky; the sea which I loved so much.

I don't remember too much about being taken, except that I was tied up and made to lie under benches awash with foul water. There were other captives, most of who made so much noise – and got beaten for it – that I felt I couldn't call out, so I was silent. One woman befriended me; she had been born a slave and was being sold on. She shared her bread with me, and told me if I was a good, clean, quiet girl, I'd be put to work in a great house, and that, she said, would be better than my own house.

Well, I was, and it wasn't. But her kindness stopped me from despairing on that foul journey.

Sometimes I imagine that someone will come to me and say, there's been a decree – all slaves are to be freed and returned home. I imagine my journey home and rushing up the steep little path from the beach. 'Mother, you'll never guess!' And however long I'd been away she'd come running, with her hard little hands, her wiry dark hair tied back, her cheeks red from tending the fire.

Of course it will never happen. Apart from anything else, I don't even know the name of the island where I grew up. It was just 'the island' and the nearby town was just 'town' and the sea was just the sea. I could never find my way home now, even if I was allowed to.

Chapter Nine

Is there a more spoiled and adored child anywhere than Astyanax, Hector and Andromache's son? For one thing, he's the heir to all of this, so his name 'King of the City' is most appropriate. None of Priam's children by Hecuba has yet had a son, so he's unique.

But really, the way they go on, you'd think there was no other child in the world. Every step in his development is discussed and passed round the palace, every smile, every gurgle, is cooed over and talked about, even by the slaves. Any sound that just might be talking is proclaimed almost from the watchtowers. Did he say Dada? Oh, I'm sure he said Dada. And yesterday he was surely trying to say Granddad.

I can't remember it too well, but I'm sure that at his age – he's just over a year – little Larisa was babbling away. But of course, she was just a village child, and no one took any notice of her.

He's not walking yet, though he's at that stage where he looks as though he's about to, at any moment; and what a fuss that causes! 'There you go, little man! Oh, just look at him! Those strong little legs!' says his mother.

'He'll be a warrior, like his dad, that's for sure!' says a slave. 'I've never seen such a strong baby!'

'He'll be running around at any moment!' says

another. Maybe they know that flattery of her son is the best way to keep in Andromache's good books.

There was another baby here until last year. He'd been born to one of the kitchen slaves, a black woman from Nubia, and the man she slept with, who worked in the armoury, repairing weapons. No one minds too much if slaves have babies – after all, they grow up to be slaves who've cost their masters nothing except their upkeep. And little children can be put to work surprisingly early. Kara called her little boy Hilarion – 'joyful', because he was. With his golden skin, great brown eyes and halo of curls, he was an exceptionally beautiful child, and everyone in the kitchens adored him. When he was tiny, he'd either be asleep in a cradle by the great fire, or his mother would perform her tasks with him wrapped in a shawl at her breast. He started to walk – quite early, if I remember – and to babble away in charming little sentences. He used to play around in the corners of the kitchen, with the dog or with the kitchen cats, smiling up at everyone with his big happy smile.

Then when he was five years old, a message came from the Great Hittite Emperor, far away in the north-east. He'd heard of the unusual beauty of this boy, and he wanted a decorative page boy at his court. Troy is actually subject to the Emperor, though most of us aren't aware of it in everyday life. The boy had to go hundreds of miles away. I watched him, getting into the cart that had been sent to take tribute to the Emperor. I don't think he had any idea what was happening to him. I remember him turning round in bewilderment, hand stretched out to his mother, who was being held back by two other slaves. He made his long journey like a piece of baggage, squashed in between bales of linen cloth, stacks of bronze spears, stirrup-jars of wine.

Kara was desolate. Her warm black skin turned grey with grief. For months, she performed her tasks with tears running down her cheeks. The kitchens became a silent and sad place, as if a death had happened.

Nowadays, Kara has regained her cheerfulness, at least on the surface. But she isn't with the man from the armoury any more, and someone said that she's determined to have no more children – she couldn't stand the grief of seeing them sent away.

Lady Helen hasn't been seen for some days now. The rumour is that she's having another miscarriage. Paris, who is desperate to have a son, must be devastated. I can't help wondering whether her miscarriages are just the workings of fate, or of the bitter-smelling medicine in the blue glass vials.

Chapter Ten

Cassandra and I are with Andromache this morning. Andromache says she needs Cassandra to help her with restoring a couple of grand ceremonial robes that Hecuba has passed down to her. With the war, it's been hard to get supplies of new linen, wool and gold thread; old garments have to be shaken out of the chests where they've been stored, dusted, mended and made good. Cassandra isn't that skilful with her needle, and half a dozen slave women could do the job more usefully, but I suspect that Andromache is just asserting her superiority over Cassandra. Cassandra and Andromache aren't the best of friends, though they like each other more than either of them likes Lady Helen. Andromache, the daughter of a king, might have expected she'd marry a king, but instead she's married into a family where the king, though he's white haired, seems more vigorous than ever. And she's also subject to Hecuba as well. She can expect to be queen some day (why, when I think this thought, does my heart do a lurch?). But she isn't there yet. And Cassandra has lost her position as the baby of the family and Hector's favourite now. I think she was a little jealous of Andromache, when she married Hector.

The heavy robe is laid out over a couple of stools. We've examined the damage. There are some moth holes, and the fringe has come loose in places. It's a tiered dress and the bottom tier is draggled and torn and will need to be replaced. I've been given the task of unpicking it. Andromache and Cassandra have got bored with the task of course, and Andromache is showing Cassandra a box of loose glass beads. They are talking about what to do with them, but probably a slave will have to do the actual work. Two of Andromache's slave girls sit in the corner, patching some linen pillow-covers. They get on with their work silently and doggedly.

Andromache hears me making a ripping noise that she thinks is too loud for this delicate fabric and calls out to me to take more care. Well, I'm doing my best, considering fine needlework is something I've never learned. Our garments in my old home were woollen, patched and darned, cut down, reused, until they fell to pieces. I imagine that now I'd find they smelled horribly of goat or dried fish.

It's a dusty, overcast, oppressive day outside, the kind of day when everyone gets bad-tempered and restless. Suddenly the door swings wide open and in comes Hector. He's been exercising his horses on the plain and is wearing riding boots and leather britches. He's covered in dust, and yes, from the look in his face, we can see he's in a bad mood. He nearly falls over a stool and snaps at Andromache for leaving it so near the door. When Hector gets into a bad temper he goes quiet and grim-faced. It's worse than shouting, somehow. I see the two slave girls exchange glances and then get up silently and creep out of the room. I can see they've done this before.

But it means that the only slave around is myself. And though I'd like to get up and go, I can't.

'Where have those damn women got to?' mutters

Hector. His fine profile is sulky and his brown curls are greyed with dust. 'I need a wash.'

'Eirene, fetch a pitcher of water,' says Andromache, though I'm not hers to order about and Cassandra shoots her a resentful glance.

'And I need a drink. That plain's a dustbowl at the moment.'

'And wine,' adds Andromache. Though no one cares how I'm going to manage a big earthenware water pitcher and a decanter of wine all at once.

I manage it somehow. We slaves do. And though I'm not Hector's servant, I have to pour the wine into a cup, and the water into a basin. I kneel before Hector and he thrusts out his feet to me to unlace and remove his boots. He doesn't expect me to take off his riding trousers, luckily, but he gets to his feet, wriggles out of them, and waves to his wife to hand him a linen day tunic. I avert my eyes at the sight of all this muscled manpower. Not that I haven't seen a naked man before, but somehow, in Andromache's chamber, the proximity is a bit close, especially as his rage fills the room like poisonous fog.

I have to clean his feet with a linen towel, then wring it out and pass it to him to clean his hands and face. He's muttering all the time, '...just can't go on like this. The beasts are getting no exercise, all my best grooms are ending up in army camps, chariots in a terrible state of repair, it just isn't good enough...'

Andromache and Cassandra exchange wry glances over his head, and Andromache comes and bends over him where he's sitting, stroking his hair gently. He leans a little into her caress, but then pulls himself away.

'Where's the boy?'

'He's with his grandparents.'

'He spends too much time there. They spoil him.'

'Darling, they love him.'

'I'm sure they do, but it's not good for him. See to it.'

'Yes, darling,' says Andromache, humouring him. But he isn't finished with us yet.

'It's madness out there these days. All those men, drunkenness, thieving, Zeus knows what. Cassandra, you're not still gadding about over the plain, are you?'

Cassandra, seeing the direction in which his thoughts are heading, stiffens. 'I have to go to the temple. I'm a priestess.'

'Not yet, you aren't.'

'Well, I haven't been consecrated yet, but Father says...'

'Well, Father must just say something else. It isn't safe for you.'

'But I never go on my own. Father sends guards with me.'

'Guards!' sniffs Hector. 'There was a gang of drunken Dardanians on the loose this morning. I had to send my own men to round them up. One or two guards aren't going to save you if that lot took it into their heads to rape you.'

'I've never had any trouble so far, Hector. They respect me.'

'Respect! There's no respect these days. No, one priest in the family is enough. I shall talk to my father about getting you married off.'

'Hector! Please do no such thing!'

He turns to her, and speaks more gently, though I don't

think his crossness has dissipated, but has just mutated into that kind of angry reasonableness which is worse than fury.

'Cassandra, dear, these are not ordinary times. In the old days, it might have been fine to have you tucked away in the temple, honouring the gods and what have you. But things have changed. We can't do what we want any more. You need to be safe. And the safest thing is for you to be married.'

'You mean, *you* can't do what you want any more,' says Cassandra mutinously. 'But we need to please the gods more than ever. You can't stop me.'

This is a challenge, a dangerous thing to issue to a man in a temper. Andromache stands up, makes a warning gesture to Cassandra, and says soothingly, 'Well, we don't need to do anything straight away. After all, you'd have to find exactly the right husband for Cassandra, wouldn't you?'

Cassandra is rigid with her own anger. I try to get us out of the room, but as I'm whispering, 'Madam, I think we should…' Andromache who has the same idea, takes Cassandra by the shoulders, and propels her out of the door. 'Just leave things alone for a while,' she says to Cassandra.

But that's almost worse for Cassandra. She's working herself up into a state now, and I think how she's seeing it is that Andromache and Hector are ranged against her. I try to calm her, but to no avail.

'I shall go and see my brother Helenus,' she says, storming off. I run after her, trying to keep up with my shorter legs.

Helenus is also a priest of Apollo, and he serves at the

small Apollo temple just inside the walls. I'm nervous about finding him there in so many ways – there is something about Apollo and my mistress which I don't understand yet, and which frightens me.

Fortunately, though, we don't have to go down to the temple to find Helenus today. He's standing in the great hall chatting to some of Hector's men, who've come back from the horse-breeding grounds with him.

He sees the fury in Cassandra's face, and takes her into a quiet corner.

'Very well,' he says, 'what is it? What's happened?'

And it all comes out in a rush. 'It's not fair, Helenus, just because he's in a bad mood, he says I'm not going to be a priestess and then he says that I have to be married, and Father promised me I wouldn't have to be married, I don't want to...'

He waves a *calm down* hand in the air. 'Start from the beginning, now,' he says soothingly. It's odd looking at him, Hector's eyes – and Hecuba's too – but he's slender and willowy. With his pale face and thin features, the eyes look darker and deeper set. He listens to Cassandra's story. 'Well, it would seem to me that the best thing you can do is to let our brother recover from his bad mood. You'll find he's probably forgotten it already.'

'Hector doesn't forget things.'

'Perhaps not, but I don't think he'll persevere with this. I'll have a quiet word with Father. It might be possible to see about getting you consecrated soon.'

The truth is that if it hadn't been for the war, Cassandra would have been dedicated to the temple already, and living out there, in a quiet grove with a few fellow priestesses. But this dreadful war has changed so many plans.

'I should be in the temple now,' she mutters.

And something shocking happens to me just then. For one of those images jumps into my mind, of the temple, the little Apollo temple in the citadel. Something unspeakable is happening and it's happening to Cassandra. Almost as soon as it's come, the image has vanished, like dirty water swirling down a drain, but it's left an imprint in my mind which I can't shake off.

For a moment, I stand there rigid. Cassandra doesn't see me, but Helenus does, and a quizzical look passes over his face.

He calms Cassandra down, and after a while she goes off. I make to follow her, but before I can go, he's grabbed me by the arm.

He pushes me against the wall, and holds me there, looking into my eyes.

'Well?' he says. 'Eirene, isn't it?'

'What do you want?'

'You know what I want, I think. Does my sister know?'

'Know what? Let go, you're hurting me. Sir.'

'That you have the Sight. You do, don't you?'

'I don't know what you mean.'

'You do. You know perfectly well. And it isn't good, is it?'

He's really hurting my wrist now. I try to wriggle away.

'What's happening to this city. It isn't good…'

I can't help gasping out, 'And to my mistress, Sir. The god Apollo. I'm worried.'

He lets go of my arm. He doesn't make me explain.

He says, 'The Sight means that one of the gods has a hand on your shoulder. Have you thought about who that may be, and why? It can be for good, or it can be entirely for evil. Just pray that in your case it'll be for good. As for Cassandra, I'll do what I can for her. But you're right. If he wants her, he'll get her. And no, that isn't good, either.' He sighs. 'Look after her, Eirene.'

Chapter Eleven

I'm distracted all day with what Helenus has said, and this afternoon, as I sit with a crowd of us, spinning flax, I'm going over and over it. No one seems to notice that I'm not joining in the conversation.

I remember in our village, there was an old woman who was reputed to have the Sight. She was a fearsome creature, with grey hairs on her chin and fingers like claws. People were terrified of her. She would stand at the door of her hut screaming out dreadful things – I don't know if they all came true, but some of them did. (Well, in a fishing village, people are going to be drowned from time to time.) Sometimes the bad boys threw stones, not quite at her, but near her. I think actually that she was mad.

I don't think I could have had the Sight when I was younger. Otherwise I would have stayed away from the seashore that day. But I do remember how it started.

I'd been a slave for a year or so – I was about nine. And one night I had one of those dreams that stays with you. I dreamed I was a priestess of Athene. I dreamed I lived on a high hill, looking over a plain far below me, silvery with olive groves. In the dream, I planted marigolds and fed crumbs to singing birds. The temple, shining white, was in the distance.

When I woke up, I couldn't get the dream out of my

head for days. Even now, it still comes to me sometimes like a real memory. And it was after that that the strange things started happening.

We were assembled for one of the family gatherings in Priam's chamber. I was standing behind my mistress and Helenus. Hector had just come in – in his riding gear, just like today – but this time he was in a good mood. He'd been training a special horse, and this horse had really been doing well that day. 'The speed! The strength! You've never seen anything like it! And you hardly need to give him orders; he just seems to understand. Going to be our champion, I think.'

And then, I heard myself saying, softly. 'But the horse is dead.'

My mistress didn't hear – she was clapping her hands with excitement at what Hector was saying. But Helenus did, and I saw his head turning slightly towards me.

And it was only ten minutes or so later, that a dishevelled and upset groom burst in; this wonderful horse had been grazing by the roadside when a snake had bitten him, and he'd died almost immediately.

In the middle of the confusion that followed, Helenus turned to me.

'Now, I wonder why you just said that.'

Many things went through my mind very quickly. Though I was only young, I knew instinctively that it wouldn't be a good idea to tell the truth, which was that I'd just *known* when Hector talked about it, that the horse was dead. I remembered the mad old woman, the boys throwing stones. I didn't understand then about all the implications of knowing such things, but I knew I had to keep quiet.

I said, 'The groom was talking about it. He was in the courtyard when I crossed it.'

Helenus gave me an odd look. 'Very well.' And nothing more was said.

After that, any of the odd dreams I got, or the thoughts I had, I kept to myself.

Do I have the Sight? I never thought so. I'd always imagined that someone with the Sight would see all the future as clearly as they see the past, which is why I never thought I had it. Not these strange incomplete snatches of thought, these disjointed images. If this is the Sight, it doesn't seem like a very useful thing to have.

But if it is the Sight, and if I do have it, then why?

By the evening, after that day of bad temper, Hector is in a good mood again. The family gathers in the great hall for dinner – Priam's children by Hecuba, and by the concubines, all those sons and daughters and sons-in-law and daughters-in-law. It's like a small tribe. A poet sings stories of great Trojan victories in the past, of wild-eyed heroes of the plain and their flashing swords, of battles and slaughter and glory. There's plenty of food, too, in spite of all the shortages, fresh meat and new bread, figs and apples and raisins. My stomach rumbles as I stand against the wall watching, ready to help my mistress.

But we slaves have this down to a fine art. The slave who has cut slices of meat from a great haunch of boar meat has cut a few extra slices which we snatch from the plate as he slips past close to us. Baskets of bread come near to us on their way round the hall. We've mastered the art of chewing with as little movement of the mouth as possible.

The King sits, of course, in the centre of the great table, on his chair inlaid with ivory panels of leopards and eagles. His white hair gleams on his shoulders like a silvery cloak. Hecuba, by his side, looks as young as a girl in the candlelight. Paris sits in shadow, restlessly shredding bread between his fingers. Hector, with his beautiful head and dark curls, dominates the conversation, as ever. He's telling an anecdote about a chariot race, years ago. Andromache, tall and gracious with her grey eyes and dark hair, leans against him, adoringly. My mistress looks beautiful too. It takes me a little aback, how beautiful she's become. I see her at her worst, I suppose, rumpled and red from sleep, spots on her chin, greasy hair that needs me to wash it. But today, her skin is clear and her dark golden hair shines. When she stands, she's tall and elegant, with her long slender bones and graceful wrists and ankles. I know she thinks she's gawky and ungainly, but she isn't. I must find a way of telling her this.

Undoubtedly, they are a handsome family, these sons and daughters of Priam. The light of candles and torches shimmer in the great hall, on the frescoes of warriors and goddesses, on the carved furniture, on the high coffered ceiling. It feels as though they have been here for ever and will be here for eternity. Even though Priam came to the throne after a fierce battle with his brothers, you'd never guess that from the tranquillity and serenity of this evening.

Suddenly there's a disturbance at the door. Slaves jump to attention, the door swings open. After a little flurry and fuss, there's silence. In the doorway stands Lady Helen. She's wearing a simple white linen dress that shows her creamy arms and shoulders and the curves of her breasts. Her dark shimmering hair hangs loose around her shoulders. There's a slender gold diadem on her brow and dangling gold earrings, no other jewellery. Her eyes seem larger and more lustrous than it's possible for a woman's eyes to be. Her beauty suddenly makes all the other beauty in the room seem tawdry and dull.

She smiles as she enters. 'Forgive my tardiness, Father,' she says directly to Priam, in her soft, husky voice. 'But may I still join you?'

Priam has leapt to his feet. 'My dear daughter! Of course! No gathering is complete without you,' he says. 'A chair for the Lady Helen, quick!'

It's not possible to see the faces of the other women. But Paris looks bashfully pleased.

Of course Lady Helen doesn't gnaw great hunks of boar meat. I notice her as the evening goes on sipping her wine from a golden goblet and delicately nibbling a few raisins and some bread.

Chapter Twelve

It's Madam's day to visit the temple on the plain and make sacrifice. I have a tense feeling in the pit of my stomach.

'Please, Madam, shouldn't you listen to your brother and stay home?'

'What are you talking about?'

'Well, the danger.'

'What danger?'

'The...the danger the Lord Hector talked of.'

'Oh, don't be so stupid. Anyway, it's none of your business.'

'But, Madam, suppose...'

'Suppose what?'

'Just suppose...something bad happened?'

'What something bad?'

But I don't know. I just know that my stomach is in a knot.

'Oh, you're hopeless,' she says. 'Now get my robes out and don't waste any more time.'

I remember when I first came to Troy how beautiful the plain around the city was, with the blue of flax fields like reflected sky, the silver curve of the river Scamander lined with drooping willows, the little farms with twirls of smoke coming from cooking fires, the sound of horses rushing over the windy acres, Mount Ida misty in the distance.

Now all that's changed. Instead of the blue shimmer of flax, there's the black and grey and brown of endless tents. Instead of sweetly scented wood-smoke, there's the rank greasy residue of hundreds of camp fires. The elegant willows by the river bank have all been chopped down for fuel, and the river runs thick with filth. Men have to walk miles now to find a clean spring – their only consolation is that all this filth is running down towards the Greek camp. The wind blows harsh and gritty, and the pathways are sticky with mud. Mount Ida is usually hidden behind a veil of yellowish fog.

In spite of all this, and in spite of Hector's misgivings, we aren't usually accosted as we make our way through the various camps. And as always we have a couple of the King's men with us.

As we go through the gateway of the lower town, there's a beggar sitting there, just outside the walls. His grimy loincloth barely covers him, his legs are dirty and covered in sores. His head, with matted dust coloured hair, hangs down.

When my mistress passes through, his head suddenly shoots up. What he says, in an appropriately quavering voice is, 'Alms, lady, for the love of the gods!'

But then he looks at me, and I see his smile, and his hard, damson-dark eyes.

Cassandra casts him an impatient glance and walks on.

I grab her by the elbow.

'Madam!'

'What now?'

I drop my voice to a whisper, but it doesn't matter how softly I speak; he'll hear me if he wants to. 'Shouldn't you…the beggar…auspicious…I mean…'

'Well then,' she says impatiently, 'you give him something if you want to. I haven't got anything.'

I have nothing, not a coin, not a scrap of food, not a detachable piece of cheap jewellery. I look at the beggar and shrug apologetically. And he smiles up at me, his teeth white and even through the grime of his face.

And what's occurred to me is that she's seen him. For the first time, he's let her see him.

I hurry to catch up with her, and tap her shoulder. 'Madam?'

She turns and gives me a look of exasperation. 'We have to get on, Eirene.'

'But Madam…?'

'What?'

'That man…the beggar by the gate?'

'What about him?'

We both turn back to look. He isn't there any more.

'I think…I think he's…' It's very hard to get it out. She's tapping her foot in exasperation. 'I think he's…the god, Madam.'

'*What?*' Her face crazes with anger like the mask of a fury.

'I know – it seems silly. But I think he is.'

The guards accompanying us turn to give us curious looks, and then start talking together in a bored way. I imagine they think we're discussing headdresses or something.

'What *are* you talking about?'

'I...I've seen him before. He has something he wants to say to you.'

'Who does?'

'He...' I don't like saying his name. 'The Divine Apollo, Madam.'

She bends her twisted up face close to me, and grabs my wrist tightly. 'Don't ever let me hear you talking such nonsense again! You know *nothing! Nothing!* Do you hear me? If you say anything like that again, I'll have you flogged! Understand?'

There's nothing more I can say.

We cross the plain, she at an angry pace. The guard behind us leads the goat for the sacrifice, and the one in front carries the wine. We pass through encampments of men, make our way through the pitted and pockmarked earth, splash in slops and animal dung. Most of the men are sitting around, some polishing weapons or cleaning boots. There are men from all over the Asian plain, some from the far north with almond eyes, some from the south, with dark skins and dark hair, Mysians, Pelasgians, Dardanians, Thracians, Phrygians, Lycians...Oh I can't remember all of their names.

Only that for all of them here, there are just as many Greeks also gathered beneath the same sky. It's frightening to contemplate.

Yet as we pass through the Trojan allies, they're quiet, respectful. Men in groups stand to one side, men sitting down stand up to attention, or bow their heads as we pass. The danger that Hector was anxious about doesn't seem to be present here.

Cassandra lopes lightly through the mud, her blonde

hair swinging from side to side in a shimmering curtain as she hurries forward. Her priestess robes are now too short for her, she's grown so tall lately, and in spite of my darning and hemming, they do look threadbare. I shall have to hurry up and get Queen Hecuba's old robes in better shape.

And she is – I can't doubt it now – beautiful. Me, I'm too short, and with hair like a thorn bush. Probably no man and no god will lie in wait for me. And that's surely a good thing.

Eventually we come to the old wooden bridge that leads across the Scamander to the shrine. The river bank is full of camp followers washing their men's clothes. Dogs and a few scrawny cattle are drinking.

But across the bridge, we can see the trees that still surround Apollo's shrine. No one will cut them down for firewood.

Across the bridge, and we're in another world. The noise from the camps is muted, fragrance from oleander and myrtle bushes drifts over to us. The shrine is surrounded by an ancient brick wall, soft rosy-red in the morning light. The gateway is surmounted by an ancient carved stone lintel, and beyond that an arch of drooping greenery.

We come in to the outer courtyard, stone-paved. The temple guards live here in little whitewashed houses beneath the wall, but no one seems to be around today. Another courtyard lies beyond, and we go through a low doorway into silence and the sanctum of the god.

Before us is a stone cistern, and around the courtyard are scattered little altars and statues of the god. The treasury, a small wooden building just in front of the shrine, is filled to the brim with all the riches people have brought for the god, ash-hafted spears, helmets, gold basins, lapis and gold jewels, statues. Wouldn't the Greeks love to get their hands on this lot?

And then, the temple itself, overshadowed by feathery plane trees, just a rectangular building of ancient stones, with a narrow dark doorway. Only Madam and the temple priestesses are allowed inside – I must stay outside on the broad step.

She's calmed down by now, but is still cross with me. 'Eirene,' she says, coldly, 'the cleansing, please.'

I take a tin ladle from the fountain wall, and scoop up the clear, cool water, which I then pour over my mistress's cupped hands. She washes her face and hands and mutters a few words.

I'm looking around while she's doing this, for the temple priestesses. There should be six of them; a slatternly lot, I always feel; if I were in charge, I'd make sure things were better run. There are dead leaves in the courtyard and eddies of dust – nobody's swept it this morning.

The priestesses share a long single-storey house along the wall. The door is open, some washed linen hangs on a thorn bush outside – in the temple courtyard!

'Where are they?' Cassandra says to me. Behind her the guards shuffle and the little goat brought for the sacrifice tosses and shakes its head.

The oldest priestess, Ela, comes out of the door, looking slow and tousled. I go over to see what the matter is. She smells sour and unwashed, her little eyes red-rimmed in her grey face. Everyone's ill, apparently. The details I don't want to go into, but she's determined to give them to me anyway; they involve lots of vomiting and visits to the privy. Struck down, they all were, this morning. Someone must have put a bad mushroom in their stew.

Well, we can manage without them. One of the guards will do the sacrifice, as always – of course the priestess mustn't get blood on her. He'll slit the animal's throat and butcher it, then light a fire to cook it. The temple priestesses will have first go, after the god has had his share. I wonder if the old dears will be as keen as they usually are about getting their hands on all that meat today. Then Cassandra will go into the temple alone to make a libation, and utter prayers.

I don't like watching the sacrifices, though I know they have to be done. It's the only way we mortals can tell the gods that we are thinking of them and honouring them. So I stand back while all the bloody business is carried out, and the smell of burning animal fat rises up from the fire the guard has built.

'You can go now,' Cassandra says to the guards, and the two of them return to the outer courtyard, where they're probably only too relieved to gossip and share wine with the temple guards.

Cassandra and I are alone now in the temple courtyard. A bird of prey glides overhead, a faint wind rustles the trees so they shiver like glass ornaments. It's gone a little chilly. I pull my scarf around me.

And I see him again, standing under the trees, just a few feet away from us.

He's not a beggar now. He looks very young, hardly a boy. His hair is ruffled and a bit dishevelled from the breeze. With his head on one side, he's smiling a slightly rueful smile. His damson eyes seem softer today. He looks more – well – human, than he's ever been.

I say, 'Madam, I...'

She looks in the direction that I'm looking in. 'What is it?' she says impatiently.

She can't see him.

'Nothing, Madam,' I say.

She makes an impatient little noise and goes into the temple, carrying a silver basin of wine. I can't follow her in, but in the chill darkness I can make out the statue of the god, one straight leg in front of the other, kilted, eyes shining at me in the gloom.

I see her in the temple pouring out the wine, raising her hands, whispering the prayer.

And suddenly he's standing there at my side. A young man with gilt hair and a silvery tinge to his pale skin, wearing a soft, finely pleated kilt of some material with a shimmer to it. His eyes are of one single dark colour; you can't make out a distinction between iris and pupil. He smells of incense and myrtle, he smells of the green darkness of a forest, he smells of a high mountain.

I hear myself say, 'Don't be unkind to her, sir.'

He smiles down at me. Then goes into the temple, and shoulders the door shut behind him.

Chapter Thirteen

I don't know what to do. I can't go in after them. I try to listen to what's going on inside, but this is the temple of a god, and you can't press your ear to the door.

Instead, I just stand there, and over and over mutter prayers of supplication to my own goddess. *Divine Athene, save her. Divine Athene, don't let him hurt her...*But whether she can hear what goes on in another's temple, I don't know. Perhaps the Divine Artemis, whose twin Apollo is, would hear me. But would she help? She's a virgin, like my mistress. But she's also a hunter.

I wait for what seems like forever and ever. The bird of prey wheels overhead and glides round and round, calling plaintively. The wind rustles in the trees. I hear the chirrup of crickets and a small transparent lizard runs across the step in front of me. Still I wait.

Then eventually, the door is flung open, and my mistress stumbles out. She's flushed and dishevelled, and she's wiping her mouth. Her eyes are staring wildly.

'Madam!' I say. 'Cassandra!' But she doesn't reply.

I'm sure I can see *him* there, walking through the darkness in his glimmering kilt, echoing the sacred statue in his gait...But then he's gone, and I'm just conscious of a puff of air as someone – something – passes out of the temple behind me.

'Madam, please!'

But she shakes her head and looks wildly about. I hold her arm; she's gone as rigid as if she's made of sticks. I don't think she sees me.

I go over to the purification cistern and dip the tin ladle into the water, and take it over to her. She grabs it from me, and gulps it down. I don't think you're supposed to drink the water but it can't hurt her now.

'Madam, talk to me! Tell me what happened!' But she shakes her head, first pushes me away, and then grabs me by the arm and hauls me back to her. I put my arm around her, and she's still and wooden.

She won't talk, just shakes her head and flings her hair about.

I wonder what I've done; did I just let some common rapist into the temple? Should I have yelled for the guards? But no – I know *he* was no common anything, and I couldn't have kept him from the temple.

I don't know how we get her home. I call the guards and tell them she's been taken sick. One of the guards finds a horse from somewhere; I'm hauled on to it, and she's pushed in front of me. I clutch her with one arm and the horse's mane with another. I hope it's a slow packhorse – I've never ridden anything before, and it's awfully high up off the ground.

Somehow, we're back at the palace. Slaves are summoned, and my mistress is taken up to her bed. Everyone says, 'What happened?' and all I want to say – all I can say – is that she was taken ill.

She's shivering now, and I'm piling woollen blankets on top of her. She's not spoken a word.

Her mother comes into the room. I can't think what to say to her. I say the priestesses had all been taken ill too, and hope that's enough to satisfy her. I can't say I let a man go into the temple after her. I can't say I let a *god* go into the temple after her. If I say either of those things, I know I'm in serious trouble.

And in the end, Hecuba goes, leaving her daughter huddled beneath blankets. 'Stay with her,' is all she says. 'I'll look in again later.'

The doctor comes and goes. He's prescribed a cordial that someone in the kitchens will make up. He talks of shutting the window so the poisonous air of the night doesn't get in, of keeping her warm.

Should I talk to Helenus about this? He's the only person here who might understand.

But I don't feel I can. I seem to be playing a part in this that I don't understand myself. Telling anyone, even Helenus, might get me into all sorts of trouble.

So I sit in Cassandra's room, dark except for a single oil lamp, stroking her shivering back, pulling the blankets over her.

Eventually, she stops shivering, rolls over, and looks up at me. Her face is ghastly pale, and her eyes are dull. 'Oh, Eirene!' she says.

I put my arm around her, and pull her to me, and I sit there, holding her as a mother holds a child who's had a nightmare, not as a slave should hold her mistress. She says nothing for a long while, and then she gives a deep sigh.

'What happened, Madam?' I ask.

She puts her hands over her eyes, as though she's trying to blot out a memory. I don't think she's going to tell me, at first, but then, gradually, and haltingly, she does.

'When…when I saw *him* in the temple, when he shut the door, I didn't know what to think…It was all dark, and then suddenly, there was this light, just coming from *him,* you know…'

Yes, I knew. As though he held a lamp, but there was no lamp.

'And he stood there, in front of me, and I just…I just fell to my knees. I was…frightened. Of my own god. I shouldn't have been frightened, should I, Eirene? Maybe that was it; maybe that was what I did wrong…'

'No, Madam, you should always be frightened of the gods. It's safer that way. You never know what they have in store for you.'

'And then he said…he said…I was one of the most beautiful of his priestesses, and that he wished to give me a gift. I said, "thank you, sir". What else could I say?'

'You couldn't have said anything else, Madam.'

'Then he came close to me, stood right in front of me, just like an ordinary man. But I could tell he wasn't an ordinary man. His skin – looked like it was made from silver.'

'I know, Madam. Go on.'

She breaks away, and looks suddenly at me. 'You did know, didn't you? At the gate. You said it was him. How did you know that?'

'I was…just guessing. But I think he was following you. You couldn't have avoided him. So what did he say next?'

'He came close. I could feel his breath on my face. It was cool, like water. And his eyes. They were…black…

like…I don't know…polished jewels. You couldn't see into them. But he was so beautiful, his mouth, his nose, his chin; everything perfect.'

'Like a statue,' I say softly.

'But he wasn't a statue. He said he wanted to give me a gift. But then…then he said, that I had to give him something in return…And I realised what he meant…'

She begins to cry. 'What could I do? I'm supposed to be a virgin. I *want* to be a virgin. I want to serve my god. I don't want…all that. But he's my god. What could I say?'

I don't know what she could have said. The gods – the male gods, at least – don't have a good reputation for their dealings with mortal women. If they want a woman, they take her, even if the consequences for the woman are terrible. And there are so many stories of what the god Apollo has done to the nymphs or the young women he's pursued.

'Madam,' I say softly. 'Did he…did he rape you?'

To my surprise, and at first to my relief, she shakes her head. But what she goes on to tell me is almost worse.

'He said…that as my gift, he'd give me the gift of prophesy. I didn't know what to say. My brother…he has the Sight. I thought perhaps if I had it, I'd be a better priestess. And then he said, did I want it? Did I want that gift? And I said…what could I say, Eirene? I said yes.'

'You couldn't have said anything else, Madam.' No, if a god chooses to give you a gift, you have to accept. And if that gift is part of a bargain also decided by the god, then you must accept the bargain too. It might seem like a choice, but it isn't.

'Then he said…that if I took the gift, then he would

take me…He put a hand on my shoulder. It felt cold, like ice. I saw what he meant. And I was frightened. Eirene… I didn't want…I wasn't ready…not there and like that…'

'I understand…'

'And he looked into my eyes, and said it again. I had to give myself to him, there and then. It was his temple, he said. I had no choice. And I…I…'

'Go on.'

'I suppose I shrank from him. I suppose I let my fear show…And he said that…that…doing it with a god was something every woman wanted, that it would be the moment of my life, that I was fortunate to have the chance…But I still couldn't say yes. I'd never thought of doing that. Father always told me I'd never be married, so I never had to think about a strange man taking me on my wedding night. I suppose I just looked afraid…and full of…*loathing*…'

She's silent for a long time. Then she goes on, in a whisper, so low, that though I'm sitting next to her, I have to strain to hear.

'I'm frozen. I can't move. Then he takes me by the shoulders and pulls me to him. I think he's going to try and kiss me. But he doesn't. He…he…*spits*…into my mouth. Then he laughs, and pulls away. He says, my reward for being desired by him, is that I'll have the gift of prophesy. And that my punishment for refusing him is that no one will ever believe me. Oh Eirene, what shall I do? What's happened to me?'

Chapter Fourteen

I don't know how I can help her. I think the best thing that she can do at the moment is keep quiet about what she's told me – nobody else knows, so far, and I feel that's a good thing. I can say that she was struck down by the same mysterious illness that struck down the temple priestesses, and should stay in her room for a few days. I just hope that no one starts wondering why the priestesses and my mistress should have been so suddenly struck down – and wondering whether it was the anger of the god that struck them down and what for. And also, why I wasn't affected, if every one else was.

I think – though I can't say – that it was the god's work. I think he wanted the temple space cleared of everyone else, while he got on with his pursuit of my mistress. The thought strikes chill into my heart.

I shouldn't really leave my mistress, but it's early the following morning and she's still fast asleep. The meal that was left for her last night is still untouched – bread and goat's cheese wrapped in leaves, and a little flask of wine.

I take the bread and the flask of wine, and creep through the palace and down the stairs and through the courtyards. A yawning guard who knows me lets me pass through the gate.

There's still a chill on the air and the smells of smoke

and cooking have been replaced by a salty freshness that must come from the sea. Also yawning, a soft grey shawl flung over her shoulders, is the priestess of Pallas Athene's temple coming around the side of the building, a willow broom in her hands.

I can't hide, as I'm already on the temple steps. She blinks suddenly and stares at me, a middle-aged woman with grey watery eyes and soft brown hair pulled back into an untidy bun. Her name is Theano. I know many of the palace women are devoted to Athene and speak to the goddess through her, but I've never spoken to her myself.

'What do you want?'

'I…I want to make an offering to the goddess.'

She isn't smiling. 'You're a slave.'

'Yes, Madam.' Aren't slaves allowed to speak to their goddess?

'So what business have you here?'

I don't have to lie to her. 'My mistress is ill, and I want to make an offering for her recovery.'

She looks at the bread and wine I'm carrying.

'Did you steal that?'

'No, Madam.' I'm lying now. At least, not exactly, for the food was for both of us, and I wasn't hungry either.

Pallas Athene's priestess seems to me a chilly, unapproachable being, though no doubt she'd be warmer if it were one of Priam's daughters who was standing on the temple steps. Anyway, she gives me a long up-and-down look. I think she's trying to find a reason to send me away, but can't think of one. In the end, she says, 'Give me that,' nodding at my offerings.

I'd rather lay them myself on the offering plate on the

steps, but I can't refuse her. I want to make my own plea to the goddess.

The priestess takes my dish and pitcher and opens the little door set in the great temple doors. It opens with a push – she must have already unlocked it and made the first morning offerings to the goddess.

'What is your mistress's name?'

'The Lady Cassandra.'

'I never knew she was ill.'

'It came on suddenly.'

I look past her into the dark depths of the temple. A single lamp has been lit, but hardly enough to penetrate the smudgy darkness. I'm trying to see the famous and ancient statue of the goddess, the Palladian, as they call it, but I can't make anything out.

The Lady Theano gives me an impatient and unfriendly glance. 'I'll make your offering for you.'

'But...'

'The immortal goddess doesn't need a slave's prayers. Go on. Off with you.'

And she disappears into the darkness, taking my offerings with her. I have nothing left to give the goddess, but I say, 'Divine Athene, please hear me, please help the Lady Cassandra and keep her from the god's anger. She's done nothing to deserve it.'

Suddenly I hear a soft whirring sound by my ears. I turn suddenly. I can't make it out at first, but then I see it, perched on the offering dish on the steps, its soft feathers silvery in the morning light, its round topaz eyes starring unblinkingly at me.

Chapter Fifteen

Whatever is happening down at the black ships? It seems that Agamemnon, the great Agamemnon, has gone mad. We hear this morning of strange goings on – rumours brought to Priam not by his spies, but by travelling merchants – nothing hidden but happening in broad daylight.

The first thing was that Agamemnon woke up after a dream that disturbed him, jumping about and calling out wildly in his tent. His slaves told other slaves, who told the common soldiers, who told, well, everybody.

Then he summoned all of his army together, on the beach, many of them still bleary from sleep, told them they had no chance of winning the war, and they were all to go home.

Most of the men went wild with delight – they're all tired of this long drawn-out war and just want to be back with their wives and families. At home, the new lambs are being born and the spring corn is waiting to be sown. Roofs must be patched and mended after the winter, hedges repaired and fruit trees pruned. I imagine they worry about their wives and daughters struggling with these tasks. They all rushed back to their tents and started packing frantically.

Only, Agamemnon didn't mean it, and Odysseus, his clever advisor, had to rush about through the ranks, calling, 'Stop! Stop! It's just a test – it isn't true.' Eventually the men settled down, order was restored and Agamemnon came to his senses.

That was first thing this morning. But the King's madness has had a result. For it seems to have strengthened the resolve of the Greek commanders, and slowly, ruthlessly, inexorably, the Greek army is gathering itself together and preparing for an assault. This time of unnatural peace is coming to an end.

And the time of darkness is on its way; the time we've been dreading, and yet been unable to imagine, hoping that somehow, by some miracle, it would all go away, and normal daily life could continue.

Hector is delighted. For weeks he's been chafing at his father's policy of wait and see. Now there is no excuse for delay – if the Greeks are ready, the Trojans have to be too.

So suddenly, there's a frantic rushing around and collecting of armour. Everything's ready, of course – one of the results of a time of doing nothing, is that armour gets polished and straps get mended and spear points get sharpened. And polished and mended and sharpened all over again.

Hector's men assemble themselves in the citadel and the lower town – the streets are suddenly full of soldiers and horses and chariots. Word is sweeping through the encampments on the plain like a tidal wave; thousands of men, many of whom don't even speak each other's languages mustering themselves and lining up. From the battlements we can see great movements of them, dark shifting shapes of men, the glitter of thousands of spear points, horses neighing, men shouting, in a dozen different tongues. War is something you can smell, fear and excitement fermenting in the air like a toxic brew.

Cassandra still keeps to her room; and now all the confusion of assembly means that no one has much time for her. Even her mother pays only a cursory visit to her this morning. I'm glad about that for it means I don't have too much explaining to do. And meanwhile, Cassandra either lies still and rigid, or sits on a stool by her window, staring-eyed. I don't know what's going on in her mind, but I wouldn't like to be sharing it.

And I don't get the choice, either. A night passes, and now it's morning, a grey chill morning, with the hint of a sea mist in the air. I doubt that there's been much sleep over the last few hours, and everyone is suddenly busy, and all the slaves are needed to fetch and carry, to help the men get ready, carry their armour from the stores, bring bundles of arrows and stacks of spears. An ancient woman slave who can't move very much is sent to sit with Cassandra, and I find myself down in the citadel helping the wife of Gorgythion, one of Priam's many sons by a concubine, as he prepares himself. He's Hector's charioteer, an important man. She's a snappy little woman, anxious and drawn, as you'd expect, I suppose, seeing your husband, large and busy and noisy before you in the morning, and wondering if you're going to be building his funeral pyre by night time. I'm glad I don't have a man to care about.

Soon everything is ready. The waiting men, princes and foot soldiers, spear carriers and charioteers stand ready and waiting in their doorways. Messengers rush about – someone, somewhere is coordinating the advance.

The thin curl of a trumpet call spirals in the air. Dogs sniff in the gutters excitedly, knowing something is going on, but not sure what it can be. Restless horses neigh.

I'm standing just beyond the palace, before the row of houses Priam built for his sons and daughters. Slaves and noble women and workmen cluster around me, straining to see. Above me I can see the great bronze and wood palace gates. For a few moments, everything goes unnaturally still.

Then with a sudden flurry, the gates are flung open.

First comes Hector, standing proudly in his chariot, driven by Gorgythius. By the chariot walks a slave carrying his huge tall shield. Hector holds his helmet in one hand and a tall spear in the other. A sunburst pattern spreads over the shining breastplate of his armour. His face is lifted to the sky, his expression clear and noble. I wonder if he had to practise that expression in a mirror, waiting for this day to come.

Behind him, rattling and rumbling over the cobbles, three more chariots: Deiphobus, Polites, Polydorus. Then the bowmen, led by Paris, who is a brilliant archer. I don't know why this should surprise me, but it does. His armour gleams and glitters, his long dark hair streams over his shoulders, a tawny leopard skin has been flung around him like a scarf, and his helmet is tucked insouciantly under one arm. He walks with a light and dancing step, and he looks from side to side, smiling charmingly at the spectators.

As they leave the palace precincts, many of us crowd on to the battlements for a better look. We see the procession of men winding down through the citadel, new soldiers joining it at every curve of the road, aristocratic soldiers gleaming with fine bronze armour, the poorer ones armed only with what they can find, sticks and cudgels, bits of wood nailed together for shields, leather helmets. They stream through the city gates, the Scaean, the Dardanian, the West, out on to the Trojan plain, where they're joined by more men, swarming in great hordes like insects. And with the metallic glitter of breastplates, the faces hidden by the curves of metal helmets, crests tossing like antennae, they're like some monstrous new kind of insect, shining beetles, or dark ants, increased a thousandfold in size, intent and inhuman and deadly.

It takes a long, long time for the procession to wind its way through the city, to join all the hordes on the plain. But eventually, it's done. The roads of the citadel are free of men, the great gates clang shut, and only fresh piles of trodden horse manure show that men and horses have passed through.

It's only then, when a sudden and awkward silence shudders across the city, that the young wives, who've until now, been silent and stoical, start to weep. First one, then another, tremulous and hushed, and the older women, some of whom have seen all this before, go over to them, and comfort them before ushering them back into the dark doorways of their homes.

Chapter Sixteen

For the moment, I'm forgotten, not wanted by anyone. The old woman still sits at the door of my mistress's chamber, her spindle working as she sits. She won't let me in. Madam is resting, she says. I can't believe that Madam is doing any such thing, and I'd like to go to her, but the old woman has seniority over me, and I don't argue.

The palace swirls with people. And gradually, most of them, like me, make their ways up to the high battlements of the palace, where the plain stretches down and away, to the far glitter of the sea.

Except that today, the sea is hidden by mist, and the sky hangs low. I lean over the parapet, and look down, down the great unclimbable walls, and the steep thorny slope below them. The procession of men and spears and horses makes its way in a great black surge on the plain below us.

And then, in the distance, we see them, another black surge, only the faintest glitter coming off their spear points in the mist, the Greek army, coming towards us.

Slowly, slowly, the Trojan mass grows smaller, and the Greek one larger, as the great hordes inch their way towards the place where they'll meet. From this distance, it all looks gentle and unthreatening like a silent game. But I imagine that down on the plain the advance is full of noise, chariot wheels rumbling, horses neighing, men swearing and shouting at each other, chariots going awry, men tripping each other up, only half able to see where they're going beneath the great helmets with their nodding plumes.

It seems to take most of the morning for the armies to get close to each other. I don't know what the rules of battle are – when do they start to fight? Is there a plan? Who decides? All I can see, about half a mile or so away on the plain, blurred now by the encroaching mist, are the two great hordes getting within yards of each other.

And then, the great movement slowly settling itself, ripples spreading out to the men on the far fringes, they come to a halt.

The man next to me on the parapet is a middle-aged slave from the stables, one of those men who's been everywhere, knows everything, and tells you all about it. On any other occasion, he'd be a bore to avoid, but today we want to know what's going on, and he's eager to tell us.

'Look,' he says, enjoying his moment of importance. 'Neither side has the advantage, see? Both sides evenly matched. No surprise tactics there. Our Lord Hector will marshal his forces to their best advantage, the other lot'll do the same, then there'll be a challenge, that's how it'll start. Hand to hand between the champions. Menelaus'll challenge Lord Hector is my guess. Then one of them'll be dead, everyone will try and grab the armour off him, both sides, then the real fighting can start. That's the way it'll be, you'll see.'

One of them will be dead...It sounds so simple put like that.

Oh. More slaves have joined in the argument. 'It won't be Menelaus. Lord Paris is my guess.'

'What, Lord Paris, hand to hand? Never! He's a bow and arrow man, that one. And Menelaus is built like a brick wall. Lord Paris wouldn't last five minutes.'

Fortunately, someone hushes him up. The slaves shrink away into respectful silence. For there, coming up on to the battlements, is the King himself, and behind him, a plain grey shawl flung over all her beauty, the Lady Helen.

Even at this terrible moment, the King seems to delight in Lady Helen's presence. She brings out the father in him, and he's gentler and more attentive to her than I've ever seen him with his own daughter.

We stay on the battlements, but shrink back to the sides, so that the King and Lady Helen can talk without being jostled. It looks as though she's pointing out elements of the Greek army to him, though how she can make out any details at this distance is anyone's guess. And it occurs to me that somewhere among that encroaching horde, is her enraged and cheated husband, Menelaus, and that they're now nearer to each other than they've ever been since Lady Helen and Paris ran away together; all his anger gathering itself together like a boil.

And also, he's facing Paris, his wife's lover.

There's movement among the distant armies. We scramble to see what's going on. Someone thinks he can make out Lord Hector marshalling his own forces so that they're still and silent – someone must be doing the same to the Greeks, for a clear space, like an arena, has opened up between the opposing forces. It seems that the know-all who predicted hand-to-hand combat between champions has got it right.

But who is challenging whom? Now we see messengers breaking loose from the mass and making their way, running, back to the citadel. Half a mile or so to go, then through the gates, up the winding streets, up the stairs and on to the battlements. At least we're in the right place to know what's going on, for the King must be told first.

It seems an age, but eventually the first panting and dishevelled messenger has scaled the stairs, two at a time, and flung himself on his knees in front of the King.

It's to be a duel. Paris has challenged Menelaus. If he defeats – by which he means kills – Menelaus, he will keep Lady Helen for ever, and the Greeks will go home. If he loses – is killed – then Lady Helen, and all her treasures must be returned to Menelaus.

I look at Lady Helen to see how she is taking this. Her face is like a white mask.

The King looks suddenly much older. For he must have worked out, as many of us listening have done, that the bright young man with his shining eyes and his dancing step will make a poor match against the big bull of the Spartan king. And it is to get worse for him. For before the combat can start, a sacrifice must be made, and King Priam must go down to all the armies, before his sons, before his enemies, and perform the sacrifice of animals, before that of his son.

Is war always so slow? More hours inch past. Two hapless lambs, a black and a white, are found from somewhere. The royal chariot is got ready. The King is taken to the battle grounds. I'm still on the battlements, not knowing what else to do with myself, and try to make out what's going on, through a mist rolling across the plain like grey water.

The sacrifice must have been made, but the mist is making it hard to see. In the end, I go back into the palace.

The old woman still sits outside my mistress's door. 'You can't go in there,' she cackles. 'She's just been given something to make her sleep.'

'Why does she need something to help her sleep?' I say in alarm.

'Talking nonsense, she was. The Lord Helenus said she needs to be kept quiet.'

I feel alarmed by this, but I can't force my way into Cassandra's chamber.

On the other hand, if no one wants my attentions at the moment, for whatever reason, then I want to make the most of it.

The endless afternoon crawls by. Eventually, the King comes back from the plain, his hair mussed and his eyes watery. He's ushered into his room. Clearly distressed, he's said he refuses to stay there to see his son killed. No one, even his father, holds out much hope for Paris's chances.

The mist has fallen all around us now. No hope of seeing what's happening on the plain, even if I wanted to; I can hardly see the citadel walls. It's brought a strange eerie silence with it, too. If there's fighting going on, I can't hear it. It occurs to me that by now Lady Helen's fate, one way or another, might be sealed. What's going through that beautiful head of hers now?

Left to myself, I'm not sure what to do. I discover I'm feeling hungry, so I go to the kitchens. No one's on duty and the great fire is almost out. I find some bread and a flask of weak wine, and take myself away to a corner, in the quiet back-entrance. No one comes here, except maybe in the morning when they empty chamber pots, or in the evenings when they bring in charcoal for the braziers. A dark little flight of stairs leads up to the great corridor where all the princes' rooms are. I sit on the stairs, eat my bread, and start to doze off.

Chapter Seventeen

I'm almost asleep. Then suddenly the little door bursts open. I'm jolted awake and jump to my feet. The man standing there looks almost as startled to see me as I am to see him. Behind him the sea mist is pushing its way into the building like an importunate guest.

The man is Paris. He's lost his helmet, his breastplate, his fancy leopard skin. His sandals are unlaced as if someone's been trying to pull them off him. His linen tunic is gashed, and stained with blood and dirt. There's dirt all down one side of his face and one arm, as though he's been dragged on the ground. One eye is black and swollen and blood courses down his forehead and cheek.

He leans back against the wall, panting. Then he sees the flask in my hand and points to it. He makes a give-it-to-me gesture and I pass it to him. He gulps down the watered wine and makes a deep sigh. He leans back with his eyes closed. Then he opens them, and I'm surprised to see he's smiling at me.

'Well, little Eirene,' he says. 'What a shock for both of us, eh?'

'What...what happened, sir?'

'What happened? A good question. As you can see, I came off worse from the combat, but I'm still here. So unfortunately, is *he*.'

He tries to find more in the flask to drink, but it's empty.

'Shall I get you some more, sir?'

'What? No. Any moment now I shall be in the arms of my lovely wife, and I shan't need anything else.' He's silent, and then shakes his head. 'Gods, what a fool. All because I let that cursed brother of mine taunt me. Challenging that thug to a fight. How stupid can you get?'

'But you survived, sir.'

'Did I? Oh yes, so I did. Here I am. Maybe the goddess loves me after all, do you think so? It was that mist everywhere. Thicker than porridge. Couldn't see an inch in front of us. So I managed to get free of the thug, and back into the mêlée where no one could see me. And so here I am.'

Yes, it's hardly a glorious victory for Lord Paris, or for the Trojans. Nothing resolved, and all that mustering and gathering and marching to be gone through all over again.

Another slave sits outside my mistress's door. By this time, I'm really feeling quite anxious about her. But the slave won't let me in. Something to do with the Lord Helenus's orders again. The slave gives me a sideways, triumphant grin. She was a loom-slave the other day – this is a promotion for her. And a demotion for me.

And a worrying one. For there seems to be something about me that the Lord Helenus doesn't like. Does he think I'm a witch? If he does, it could be dangerous for me – witches are thrown from the highest point of the walls.

What is going on behind my mistress's door? I know she needs me, that I'm the only one who can help her, or who understands her now. Why can't they let me in?

Today's battle has ended in a stalemate. After the fiasco of Paris and Menelaus's combat, there was a little sporadic fighting among the men, but the mood of the day and the encroaching mist made it impossible to continue, and an uneasy truce was declared. Gradually, all the men come streaming home, tired and discontented and dusty. They were all geared up and ready to fight this morning, and it was all for nothing. There'll be some bad temper in their chambers throughout the city.

Hector is no exception. I hear banging and clashing coming from behind the door of his room, buckets of hot water being carried to and fro, the baby crying. Bad temper travels downwards through the ranks; Andromache's voice is raised almost in a screech, and slaves snap at inferior slaves.

The baby is still crying. The door bursts open and Andromache appears, carrying him. I imagine that Hector has said something like, 'Get that brat out of here!' I know that the baby's nurse fell down a stair the other day and broke her wrist – she won't be on baby-carrying duty for some time. Andromache's normal poise has gone, her hair is fly-away and her eyes anxious. And the more anxious she is, the more the baby cries. Poor little thing – all this coming and going must be unnerving him.

Without thinking what I'm doing, I come forward. 'Let me take him from you, Madam.'

Ouch. He's a big heavy boy and his little feet are rigid as he digs them into my hips. 'Come on now, little one,' I whisper into his soft dark hair. 'Calm down for Mamma now. Calm down...'

And amazingly, he does. The crying subsides to little

broken gasps, and then to a whimper and then to silence. Andromache gives me an odd look. She doesn't really want me to be the one to quieten the precious boy, but I have done, and she needs the space to cope with her other bad-tempered male.

Soon the little boy falls heavily asleep, his head on my shoulder. The dark curls on his head are slightly damp from all the exhaustion of crying, but his long dark lashes lie softly on his cheeks, and his breath comes easily. I wish I had a shawl to wrap him in so that I could carry him with my arms free as the nursemaid does, but I can't. I slink into Hector and Andromache's chamber, and sit quietly on a stool in the corner, almost falling asleep myself.

Gradually Hector's temper improves, as he's bathed and dressed and combed. It's not to be a quiet evening yet for him, for the King has summoned his close family to his chamber again.

Priam sits on his high chair, Hecuba by his side. Around him are ranged stools for the rest of the family. Slaves sneak into corners and sit on benches. Priam suddenly looks like an old man, so frail you could blow him away. Hecuba seems to be made of a cold hard metal as she sits by him, straight as a rod.

One by one the family trail in. Hector, Andromache. Young Troilus. Deiphobus, Polites and his new little wife, Polydorus, Helenus, tall and grave.

But not everyone's here. 'Where's my son Paris?' says the King, looking around. One or two slaves hurriedly suppress a snigger.

'Sire,' says Deiphobus, in a voice which you'd use

to calm an angry horse. 'Paris is...has asked not to be disturbed.'

More giggles from the slaves.

'What do you mean, asked not to be disturbed?'

'He is....' Deiphobus doesn't like Paris much, I think, so he's probably enjoying this, though it's a bit embarrassing. 'He is...he asked the servants to leave...he is in bed... privately...with his wife...'

Oh. So that's what's going on. Andromache raises an eyebrow, Hector fetches up a deep and irritated sigh and shakes his head,

'I see,' says the King. Then, 'And my daughter Cassandra. What of her?'

Now it's Helenus's turn. 'Sire, the Lady Cassandra is not well.'

'Come, come, she was not well the other day. What's the matter with her?'

'Just that...it's better for her to stay in her room.'

'Has she got a fever?'

'No.'

'Got the runs?'

'No, but...'

No buts. Priam has been deprived of one child this evening and isn't going to be deprived of another. 'Then fetch her. Bring her here at once.'

Chapter Eighteen

Cassandra stands in the doorway, a slave on either side of her. Poor Cassandra – I haven't seen her now for a day and she looks terrible. She's waxy-pale and red around the eyes. Her hair hangs loose and nobody's combed it for her since I last did it. Her feet are bare, and she's wearing that shapeless old rust-coloured robe that's already done duty for several palace ladies.

But it's the look on her face that cuts me to the quick – a look of blind, blank fear. I long to go to her, but I'm nursing the little King of the City now, and also, Helenus has just shot me a look. I slink back against the wall.

Priam doesn't notice – or pretends not to notice – his daughter's state. Hecuba has risen to her feet in anxiety, but the King reaches out an arm and pushes her back into her seat. Even a mother and a queen must obey a king.

'Cassandra, my dear daughter,' he says, in a studiedly normal voice. 'How good to see you. Come forward, girl, and kiss your old father.'

Cassandra goes rigid. Her eyes glaze. She lifts her hands slowly so that she stands like a suppliant statue.

I rise to my feet, still holding the baby – I can't help myself. I think she's possessed by the god.

But Helenus is at my side. He looks at me, then at her. 'Sit down!' he hisses. 'Don't go near her.'

Slowly, stiffly, Cassandra moves forward. Then it's as though she sees her father for the first time. She gives a fearsome scream. Astyanax stirs in my arms. 'Oh Father,' she says in a strange high-pitched voice. 'Oh! I can't bear it. Oh, dead, dead, like that at the altar! Oh, don't go near the altar!'

Then she stops and spins round, looks at all of us. The voice is a high screech. 'Oh Hector, don't, please don't! He'll drag your body behind him! Don't anger him! Oh Andromache, how can they make you a slave, and your boy dashed to pieces! Oh...h...'

But whatever she's going to say next is stopped, as Hector rushes over and grabs her. She stands rigid in his arms. 'Get her out of here!' he yells, and two slaves have to manhandle her and haul her out of the room, still screaming in that strange, mad call, still calling doom and death upon all the assembled family in Priam's chamber.

Chapter Nineteen

The following morning, the Trojan forces assemble themselves as they did yesterday, helmets, spears, chariots, horses. Once more, women gather in their doorways as the men wind down the streets of the citadel and make their ways on to the great plain. But today there's no crying among the women. Maybe they realise that this day of fighting must be followed by many more, and they might have to save their tears for greater horrors to come.

It's a clear day today and from the battlements we can see the line of Greeks in the distance, like a creeping black tide, with the Trojans moving towards them. Here we stand, women, old men, children, slaves and free, all now without much purpose in our lives – everything hangs on what those black tides of men will do. If the Trojans succeed, then the Greeks might go back to the black ships and leave us alone. If they lose, then it doesn't take an army long to sack a town. By this evening, I could be the property of a Greek soldier.

Of course, there's much talk about yesterday's battle – men came home the previous night full of the rashness of Paris's challenge to Menelaus, and how close Paris came to death in the combat. Paris let fly his spear to no good effect in the first moments of the fight – and then Menelaus was upon him, battering him, choking him with the leather strap of his own helmet. Then the helmet came away in Menelaus's hands, the big man fell over, and in the confusion and the swirling mist, Paris managed his fortunate escape. Some of the women are muttering that it would have been better if he'd been killed, and then 'the Greek whore' could be despatched back to her husband, leaving them all in peace.

But whatever the Trojan women think, clearly the gods want Paris left alive, as though they have a task for him still to do. I wonder what it can be.

Meanwhile, my poor mistress has been confined to her room. Two slaves are to be on duty outside, all hours of the day and night. Everyone thinks she's gone mad, and the King doesn't want a mad girl screaming about death and destruction just now. I long to go to her, but I haven't been allowed near. I haven't seen Helenus to ask why, or what it is he thinks that's wrong with me being allowed to see her – he's down in the little temple by the walls, making offerings to the god. And again, some instinct is telling me that I should keep quiet about all this, that I must try to preserve myself.

The boring slave who knows all about warfare has an audience around him, as he points across at the mêlée, over the parapet walls, but I don't want to listen. He'll be talking of the pre-battle preparations, jockeying for the best position, feints and false attacks, gathering of archers, chariots, all these things that will happen before the first blow is struck…

And somehow this must have happened, for now those two black masses of men have become one; one distant silent, swirling black stain.

How eerie a distant battle is – only the faintest of sounds drifts towards us as occasionally the wind brings us the frantic neighing of a horse, or a concerted shout from a group of men. Otherwise, we're just looking out on the windy plain, while men are killed and maimed, all far away, far, far away. Soon we'll have to deal with the reality of all this; at the moment, it's all like a bad dream. I can't imagine what it must be like to have a father, or a husband in that distant, uncanny throng.

At around noon, perhaps because they need to feel they have a task, the women of the citadel gather together to make a great offering of prayer to Athene. Everyone chooses some article that they cherish, an embroidered robe, a carved ivory spindle, a gold bracelet, an embossed drinking cup (Cassandra isn't allowed to be part of this, needless to say). All file down towards the temple, where Theano is waiting for them. This offering isn't for slaves to take part in – even if I had something to offer, I wouldn't be welcome, but I watch them gathering on the temple steps. There's a fluttering movement behind me – I turn quickly, and for a moment I think I've seen my little owl just vanishing from my sightline – but it was only for a moment, and I can't be sure.

It's starting to get dark. Colours are fading from the plain, and long clouds, grey and ochre and pink, are massing like silken streamers over the sea. And somehow, by some mysterious distant process that we can't understand, the battle is over. We see men coming back over the plain – not now in a great disciplined throng, but in ones and twos, slow and hesitant. No doubt similar groups are making their way to the Greek camp. And now we can see bodies left lying on the plain. Mule carts go out from the city. It's hard to see at this distance, but people are walking among the bodies, putting some on stretchers and others on the backs of carts. All seems so slow, so distant.

Then the first survivors reach the city, and then things start to happen fast. As the men come in, their women are rushing out to them, holding out their arms. 'Have you seen so-and-so? Is my man all right?'

The uninjured and lightly injured men come first. All are limping and dusty, and you can't always tell who are the noblemen with their bronze armour and who the foot soldiers with makeshift weapons, so grimy they all are

Today, I'm an unattached slave, and as such, I realise, I'm going to have to make myself useful. A little bandy-legged scarred veteran is sufficiently in control of things as to be giving orders to anyone and everyone who's around. I'm sent down and across the plain to the battleground. To help.

The plain I cross now in the deepening twilight has nothing in common with those childhood memories, when Troilus, Polites, Cassandra and I would toss a ball to each other and scramble over rocks. Those memories seem to belong to a different person. I wonder where Troilus and Polites are at this moment.

There are scores of us now streaming across the plain. Some people carry tarred torches, flaming against the wind. Men are coming in the other direction, some barely able to walk, supported by comrades. Some, carried on stretchers, are crying out and reaching out their hands to us as we pass. They call for water, but we have no water.

The pale pink clouds have deepened to rose and

the light has almost gone from the sky. The plain is now one great grey expanse. Sometimes we trip over bodies, men who have come so far and then collapsed. There's a chariot turned on its side, dead horses in a mound. At least, not dead, for a terrible groaning comes from one of them. I hope someone has a spear and the humanity to finish it off.

First, the stench comes to meet you. I never imagined that a battlefield would smell so bad; a blast of excrement and blood and sweat and butchery. Flies are buzzing everywhere in angry black clouds. I push my way through them and almost trip over a body. Some of the bodies are being stripped of their armour. It causes great shame to a warrior to have his armour taken from him, even through he's dead. For a hero, it should join him on his funeral pyre, for an enemy it becomes a gleefully-taken spoil. I don't think the people taking the armour are soldiers, though. I see women and even children. Maybe they used to live in the village which the Greeks have long ago ransacked.

In the dusk, you can't see bodies clearly, but sometimes the blaze of light from a flare reveals horrors, hacked off limbs, spilling guts. Here a head without a body stares up at me with wide, shocked eyes. I swallow down nausea.

Not everyone is dead, and that's the worst thing. Those who can call out are calling for one thing – water, and more water. And some are calling it in the old familiar language that I used as a child – there are Greeks here, as well as Trojans; blooded, despoiled, half-naked, there's little difference.

And here and there, a frantic woman who's raced across the plain has found the body of a loved one – I hear ghastly screams, see them scrabbling in the dust to smear their faces in angry mourning. All of this in the twilight, while the sky glows crimson for the last few minutes and the sun falls thankfully into the distant waters.

Someone is passing on orders. We are to take bodies back to the walls of the citadel, where they'll be burned. A big woman, with red muscular arms, is by my side. 'Come on,' she snaps.

She stops by the nearest body. We know it's a Trojan by the design of the little knife he still clutches in his hand. He's been wounded in the neck – blood has pumped from his chest and started to congeal in a blackish waterfall over him. If he had a helmet and shield they've already been taken. One of the men with a torch stands over us. 'Come on! Shape up!' barks the big woman, as though she's done this before. She bends down, and smartly lifts the young man up from his armpits. His head, with dark curly hair lolls suddenly down to one side.

I must pick him up by the legs. The flesh is cold already, clammy and greasy. I take hold of him by the ankles and pull, while she lifts his trunk off the ground. It's a dead weight – literally a dead weight, heavier than you can imagine. I try to settle the weight comfortably, holding him under the knees. His sandaled feet flop down against my thighs. I take a deep breath and we get going, she walking backwards, looking over her shoulder as she goes, me walking forward. The dead man seems to be looking at me. I wish someone had thought to close his eyes first. And he stinks – this nice-looking ordinary lad stinks.

It's a long way back to the citadel, and the ground is

pitted and bumpy. Several times, we have to stop, lay our body down and draw deep breaths. All the time the young man stares at me with his unblinking eyes. I wonder what the last sight was that he saw with them.

Finally, we arrive back at the hilly ridge before the city. Bodies are being laid out in rows. Before we have laid our young man down, two or three women run up to us, grab him by the shoulders to peer into his face, then breathe sighs of relief. They don't even see us. We lay him down at the end of a row, next to a guard holding a torch. People are running everywhere, hither and thither. Not far away, a huge funeral pyre is being built. But funeral pyres take a large amount of wood, and these days most of the trees on the plain have been cut down. I see men hauling beams from derelict houses and barns, others with piles of thorn bushes that won't be much use as fuel. If they'd died in the normal run of events, these young men would have their bodies cleaned and anointed with scented oils, and laid out among flowers; they would have been visited and honoured, and buried with prayers and reverence. Now they'll all be piled on a heap, with only the barest of ceremonials, and their spirits sent up blazing to the skies.

Chapter Twenty

Bodies are still waiting on the battlefield to be collected, but the big woman takes me by the elbow and looks at me as though she sees me for the first time. 'You're only a girl,' she says. 'You've done all you need to. Get back to your master and mistress now.'

Thankfully, I do as she says. My arms and back are aching so much, I doubt if I could carry another body across the plain. To say nothing of going back to all that stink and horror.

Everyone's milling around at the gates, so there's no one to notice me. In the lower town, doors, which would normally be firmly shut at this time of the evening, are flung wide open, lamps burning everywhere. People are still coming and going, injured men still being lifted into houses. I hear groans and cries and screams, and the cacophony of bewildered dogs, who don't understand what's happened, but know something has.

I make my way through the palace gates – nobody stops me – I reckon even a Greek spy could sneak in quite easily this evening and into the great hall. Now the dead are being given names – and I learn that one of Priam's sons, Democoon, was killed today, and the King is in his chamber mourning, with Hecuba, though Hecuba wasn't the mother of this young man. I hear the names of the

Greek warriors as I walk through the Trojans, I learn who was brave, who was foolish, who got killed, or nearly killed: Odysseus the wily, Ajax the Giant, and Ajax the Skilful, Idomeneus, Diomedes and ancient Nestor are still alive. I hear that Achilles is still refusing to fight, and threatening to go home. Without Achilles, everyone says, the Greeks don't stand a chance. Agamemnon is trying to get Achilles to change his mind, offering him gifts, even, it's said, returning the girl Briseis to him.

But Achilles wants to return home, to his mountain lands in Phthia, to his old father and his son and his vineyards. Who can blame him? It's said that once, long ago, the gods offered him the choice of a long, peaceful and unnoticed life, or a short and glorious one. Everyone thought he'd choose the short and glorious. But now I'm not so sure. Everything is in the balance. He might go home – and if he chooses that, then the Greeks are doomed to lose, according to their seer. All depends on that choice of one man; the city of Troy, all our fates.

Andromache is here, her hair untidy and her eyes wild. 'Where's that wretched Greek girl?' is what she's calling.

Someone pushes me in her direction and she stops suddenly and stares at me. I realise that my dress is blooded and soiled and vainly try to smooth it down.

'What in Hades have you been up to?'

'Sorry, Madam. I was helping with the bodies.'

'You've got no business helping with bodies. You're a palace slave. And I need you to look after…' She stares at my dress. 'Not like that – you're filthy. Go and get cleaned up at once. Have you got another dress?'

'Yes, Madam.' Being a palace slave I have to look

nice, and keep one dress clean – wash and wear. So there's another one, in the chest. The chest which is in Cassandra's room.

'Well, put it on AT ONCE, clean yourself up, and report to me. Now – Echemon – where is he? I need him NOW.' And off she goes, full of important tasks.

From the pump by the back wall, I clean my face and arms and feet as best I can. But I can't go round the palace in this dress; so I go to my mistress's room on the attic floor. A single slave is sitting there, by the light of a small oil lamp. He's dozing off, but he wakes up as I come near. It's very quiet on the top floor, away from all the dramas below.

The slave is a little man called Phokas, who usually works in the kitchen. Is my mistress reduced to this now – kitchen slaves to guard her?

I tell him I need to go in to my mistress's room. He pompously starts telling me about orders. Orders are orders. No one must. No exceptions.

Then the door opens and Cassandra is standing there. At least they haven't locked the door on her.

'I thought I heard your voice,' she says. I can't really see her face in the darkness, but her voice is flat and empty.

The little slave starts up again. 'Now, look here, I have my orders, and I'm sorry, Madam, but nobody must...' Oh, he's enjoying this; seldom does a slave get a chance to boss his masters about.

I decide to tackle him first. 'You may have your orders, but I have mine, from the Lady Andromache, and they're to get out of this filthy dress as soon as possible and get into the clean one which is in this room, or she'll have your guts, do you understand?'

There's a little more arguing, but in the end he grumbles that he doesn't know where he is with these people, telling him one thing then another. I slip into the room and glare at him. 'Well, I'm not changing my dress with you standing there looking at me. Shut the door, please.'

And still grumbling, he does so, and I'm alone in the chamber with my mistress, a single lamp burning on a bronze tripod.

'Oh, Eirene,' she says.

'Oh, my Lady.'

'I'm a prisoner.'

'I can see. It's not right.'

She sighs deeply. 'I'll get your clean dress. That one stinks. What have you been doing?'

I don't want to tell her. 'There's a lot happening out there.'

'I know. I suppose everyone's too busy to be worrying about me.'

'I hope so, Madam. I hope they let you go.'

'Oh, they won't do that. Not Helenus. He *knows*, I think. Let me help you off with that.'

Well, that's a first time – my mistress helping me. I wish it wasn't so. She takes the soiled dress off, and helps me into the clean one. She fastens it on the shoulders before she continues. 'I can't help it, Eirene. The things I say. *He* says them. He takes me over. I can't stop what comes out of my mouth.'

'I know that, Madam.'

'And then, when I've said them, they're still there, in my head. I can't get rid of them.'

'Pray to him, Madam. Implore him to let you go.'

'He won't do that. He doesn't change his mind. And, oh, it's so dreadful. We're all going to die, Eirene.'

'Don't say that.'

'But it's true. All of us. At least,' she looks at me, 'perhaps not you. Perhaps you'll live. But me, Eirene. And the worst thing is, when it comes to it, I shan't mind dying because it'll be better than what's happening to me…Oh don't cry.'

I haven't shed a single tear on this day of dead young men. But I find I'm crying now. And the worst thing is, that somehow, and I don't know how I know, I know that she's right.

Chapter Twenty-one

This night, there's no comfortable family gathering in the King's chamber. Instead, there's a meeting, far into the night, by a slow burning fire, in the great hall as Hector and the chief commanders gather together and discuss tactics. Today's battle was inconclusive, but it seems that Hector is convinced that tomorrow the Trojans will get the upper hand. He's confident and persuasive, and his enthusiasm will give energy to his men.

Still, it's a sad and desolate sight that meets us the next morning. Most of the bodies have been identified and shrouded by their families now; women and children sit around them, smearing their faces with dirt, tearing their robes, keening and crying. The huge funeral pyre has been completed, wood brought from wherever it can be found, and soon the bodies will be laid on it, priests will recite prayers, and then a torch will be plunged into the midst. In the distance we can see a plume of smoke which suggests that the Greeks have already done the same thing.

A great wall of smoke and flames, the stench of burning flesh, greasy ashes flying everywhere, even over the palace walls. Nobody wants to go and stand on the battlements today. I'm worried that when the pyre dies down, no one will be there to perform the final rites properly – to damp down the ashes with wine and the proper incantations, so that bones can be taken from the ashes, wrapped reverentially in linen, then buried. Without those rites completed, the spirits of all those young men will be trapped here forever, endlessly wandering the Trojan plain. I grieve for them.

I seem to have acquired a new job as Astyanax's nurse, and he's in a restless, fractious mood, so it's all I can do to keep him quietly entertained. No singing, no games, or course – the palace is in mourning.

The day drags on. Another silent, eerie day, of hours impossible to fill. Sometimes people report on what's going on. The battle can't be seen today, even from the battlements. It seems that Hector's plan, which was to get as close to the Greek camp as possible, and demolish their defences, might be working. But we shan't know till the evening.

And then, finally, this day, too is over. The first news is triumphant. Hector comes in ahead of all the men, grimy, blood-spattered, bruised; his huge shield nicked and dented. Still he's laughing and exultant. It seems that not only has he managed to storm the defensive wall that the Greeks built around their camp, he's also managed to get among the Greek ships and set fire to many of them. He's left the Greek camp in confusion, bodies piled everywhere.

But there is a price to pay. More deaths, even among the successful Trojans. Among them, Gorgythion, Hector's charioteer, whom I helped to get ready just the other day, killed by Hector's side; another son of Priam's dead. And more Trojan dead will have to be brought over from the battlefield. In the temporary truce that closes each day's fighting, detachments of already exhausted men must make their way back to the Greek camp and collect the bodies of their comrades and whatever bits of armour haven't been looted. Tomorrow there will be another funeral pyre as high as today's.

In spite of all this, Hector is convinced that at last the tide is on the turn and that it's only now a matter of time before the Greeks are driven away. 'We've paid a price for this victory,' he says, in his wife's room that evening. 'But it'll be worth it. You'll see; we can't lose now. In a week or so, we'll have our city back, and then we can live out the rest of our lives in peace, my darling one, with our son.'

There are only two flies in this particular ointment. One is the words that Cassandra, possessed by the god Apollo, has spoken. Everyone has dismissed them as mad ravings, but I can't.

And there's something else, something that happened this morning on the way to the battlefield. Helenus, who is also present in Andromache's chamber this evening, witnessed it, and reminds his brother of it now. It seems that as the men made their way across the plain, a huge eagle flew overhead in front of them. In its talons was a great snake – still alive. As the bird flew, the snake wriggled and lashed out furiously. It was a match of equals. And in the end, the eagle had to let go of the snake, sending it plummeting to the ground, from where it managed to slither away.

'If you can't see the significance of that, brother,' says Helenus quietly, 'then you're a fool. You may think you have the Greeks in your claws, but you don't. There's still life in them. There's still danger for you. The message couldn't be clearer. Ignore it at your peril.'

'Oh yes?' scorns Hector. 'It's all in the birds, is it?

Well, you keep watching your birds if that's what you want; if they're flying upside down or inside out or back to front, or whatever. I prefer to put my trust in Almighty Zeus, and *he*, let me tell you, my priestly one, is firmly on our side! Just you wait and see!'

Chapter Twenty-two

Impossible to remember a time, though it was only a few days ago, when mornings didn't start this way – men arming and preparing themselves and winding in procession through the citadel and on to the plain, the shouts, the trumpet calls, and then the eerie silence after they've marched off towards the Greek ships.

But fragments of news come across the plain to us; some wounded men returning, or slaves who've been taking fresh supplies of spears and arrows to the battlefield. Hector is continuing his unstoppable advance, it seems. Again he's down by the Greek ships, aiming to destroy as many of them – and Greek soldiers, too – as he possibly can. They tell us of the smell of burning tar and wood as the black ships catch fire, and the great hissings and splashes as the Greeks try to quench the flames. It seems that Hector's confidence has been justified.

Until noon, that is, and then suddenly things seem to change. I'm sitting – as I must these days – in Andromache's chamber. All the women are working at their looms, only the rattle of the wooden frames and shuttles breaking the silence. The King of the City is at my feet, absorbed with a pile of wooden bricks. He puts one on top of another, knocks then over, and looks up at me with a triumphant giggle. I pile up a tower of three for him, and he knocks those down too. He throws back his little head and laughs joyously.

And then someone bursts into our chamber. 'My lady!' he calls. 'It's Achilles! Achilles is coming!'

Shuttles are dropped with a clatter, stools pushed back scraping the polished floor. Carefully rolled up balls of coloured wool run across the floor, this way and that, untangling in vivid angular patterns. Everyone rushes to the door, slaves and mistresses, no one waiting for orders. I scoop up the heavy unresisting weight of the King of the City. He thinks this is a new game.

Along the corridor, up the stairs. Everyone has the same idea. The little king bounces heavily against my hip. If ever there was a case for a child to be walking, this is it.

We reach the palace battlements and peer over. No silences now, a great noisy surge of men and chariots and horses. It seems the Trojans are retreating from the Greek camp and moving back to the city, impelled by some unseen force.

And then the whisper of *'Achilles'* goes along the battlement walls.

Now I see it – the great chariot breasting its way through the dark surge of men, like Poseidon through the waves. The chariot, Achilles's charioteer clutching the reins in both hands, is larger and more glittering than any mortal chariot could be. And the first thing to strike you are the horses – three, not the usual two. Two of them are silver, with glittering manes and great swishing tails, their hooves pounding on relentlessly. And the other – a little smaller, but no less strong – is a golden colour. I've heard of these horses, though I never imagined I'd get to see them. Two are immortal – Balios and Xanthos – the gift of Poseidon to Achilles's father Peleas. And the third, Pedasos, though he looks as fine as his companions, is a mortal horse. He was brought back by Achilles one day, heartbroken at losing his master, but the immortal ones comforted him in horse language, and now the three are inseparable.

And then, behind them all, standing in the chariot, waving a great spear – who could miss him? We know him by the armour – people who know say that only Achilles has such armour, a gift from the gods to Achilles's father Peleus at his wedding; a great patterned breastplate of bronze inlaid with silver and gold and lapis – so they say – we just catch the glitter of it in the sunlight – and a great bronze helmet, with a deep blue plume, hiding his face. It's shocking, but also strangely exciting, to be seeing the great Achilles like this.

Men and horses are swirling around, arrows flying, spears flashing, but nothing seems to be able to stop him. He comes so close that we can see the embossed pattern on his helmet quite clearly, hear the neighing and panting of the horses. 'He's going to storm the walls!' says someone. Then the great chariot wheels round, races below the ridge and soon is out of sight.

The walls are thirty feet high and thick. They go round the upper citadel, on three sides, and then are abutted by the smaller walls of the lower city which laps on to the citadel. The lower city would be easy to storm, but it would take a large number of men to do it. There's only one place where the stone walls of the upper citadel could possibly be breached, on the south-western flank, near an ancient fig tree, where they were damaged a few years ago by a small earthquake and haven't been properly repaired. But even that wall has a slope on it that makes it almost impossible for one man to climb, especially if others are on the battlements, raining down stones upon him.

We wait, quietly, anxiously on the palace roof. Noises come up from below, everyone shouting. The little King of the City becomes fretful and snivels and wriggles and kicks against me.

And then after an age of waiting, the chariot hurtles into our view again. If its rider tried to storm the palace walls, he must have failed, though he's still triumphantly waving his spear around him. Men close in around him. If there's to be a battle it's to happen close to us, so close that we could almost throw things down on the combatants. Trojans and Greeks are mixed, rushing and plunging and shouting.

And then all at once, another cry. *Hector!* He too comes in a chariot, though driven by mortal horses, across the plain, shouting. His coming seems to divide the tidal surge of the armies; there's a sucking of men away, like a wave, towards him, Greeks who are trying to kill him, and Trojans who are trying to kill them. There's a sort of ruthless pattern to it all.

Things happen quickly now. There's a terrible animal scream from the chariot below us – the great golden horse rears and stumbles, blood fountaining from its side. The silver-white horses rear too, but they're not hurt; they can't be; they're immortal. The chariot lurches; the charioteer struggles to regain his balance. The warrior in the splendid armour lurches too. Then suddenly, he's struck. He loses his footing and falls to the ground. As he falls, a swarm of men descend on him, some to defend him, some not. I hear a triumphant cry and the great helmet with its blue plume is wrenched from his head and waved in the air. The man who was wearing it is struggling to his feet, shaking the brown hair down his back.

And another whisper goes up around the battlements. *That's not Achilles!* Who is it? The answer comes soon. *It's Patroclus!* Achilles's dear friend. But what is Patroclus doing in Achilles's armour? No one can answer that question.

Hector is urging his chariot through the mass. As he approaches Patroclus, he leaps down from it and charges towards him. His horses rear up in the crowd, trampling men beneath them. The other chariot lurches here and there, out of control, one horse in its dying throes and the other two swaying and trampling around it.

Patroclus, waving his huge spear, has risen to his feet now. He seems to be unscathed by the blows he's received and by the fall. He ploughs his way through, stabbing and thrusting with the spear as he goes. Men fall. I can see that these men are going to die.

I remember those days when the young princes of the city and my mistress and I used to go off down to the beach, how after a while, the boys would get tired of playing decorous ball games, and they'd start fighting. Bits of old driftwood became spears, they held imaginary shields in their bent arms. 'You're dead! I got you there!' one would cry. And the other would say, 'No, you didn't! I got *you!* You're dead.' Sometimes, by a sort of tacit agreement, one would agree to be dead, and fall down, clutching his stomach and moaning. Then he'd jump to his feet again, and the fighting would continue. I didn't realise then that these play fights were rehearsals for real wars, with men losing their guts and screaming like stuck pigs. Somewhere in this mess Troilus and Polites are playing those fights for real now.

Then we see Hector, pushing his way through, coming close. The others part around them, drawing back fearfully, stumbling over bodies, so that a kind of open arena spreads out around the two.

Now they stand poised, facing each other. Patroclus looks around, as though he hasn't quite worked this out. With a great cry, Hector raises his spear, comes forward and jabs hard. He finds the tender place below the breastplate, the unprotected belly, and drives it home.

That's all it takes, a quick and violent thrust, and a man just off-guard for a moment. Patroclus falls without a cry, but with a great gasp. His armour clanks and crashes as he falls backwards. Hector stands over him, plants a foot firmly on his chest to steady himself, and then tugs the spear out. Blood fountains from the wound. Patroclus's spirit goes from him. It's all over.

Hector is triumphant. Someone has handed him the great blue-plumed helmet and he waves it in the air, his foot still on Patroclus's chest.

Patroclus was kind, so they said; the only person who could hold back Achilles's anger and calm him down. Everyone liked him. What is there now to stop Achilles's rage?

The battle continues for the rest of the afternoon, around the city, but Andromache can't bring herself to watch it any more and calls us back to the chamber. Not much weaving is done that afternoon, I think, though women pretend to be busy. We can hear the clamour of the fighting, and from time to time, someone comes to tell us what's going on. In triumph, Hector has discarded his own armour, and put on Achilles's. I don't like this – it sends a shiver down me; when confidence turns to bravado, the gods become angry. There's been a struggle for Patroclus's corpse. The Trojans would hack it to pieces and feed the bits to the dogs, I imagine, but the Greeks wanted to get it back to their camp so he can be given proper burial, and in the end, they've succeeded. There must be some small consolation in all this for Achilles. But I wouldn't want to be the one to tell him.

Another evening comes around. And once more we hear the toll of the dead. Sarpedon is dead, handsome, graceful Sarpedon, rumoured to be the son of Zeus himself. If even Zeus's son can die, what help is there for lesser mortals?

Although the Trojans still have the upper hand, this wasn't quite the day of decisive victory that Hector had anticipated. Menelaus, Agamemnon, Odysseus, Idomeneus, Diomedes and the giant Ajax still live. Some of the ships have been burned, but most of the fleet remains. The defences round the Greek camp are probably being patched even now.

But still, there are those thirty-foot impregnable walls. There are all Troy's allies, spreading out over the plain. There's Troy's leader, now clad in armour from the gods.

That evening, something awful happens. Cassandra manages to 'escape' from her prison and runs screaming through the corridors before she's caught, taken back to her room and given a powerful sleeping draft to quieten her down. What she was screaming about was fire and destruction for Troy, the impregnable walls being breached, men killed, women taken...On this day when Troy feels it is close to victory, no one must hear words like these.

Chapter Twenty-three

What goes on that night in Achilles's camp? Who was the bearer of the terrible news? Did Achilles guess as he saw the man coming towards him, ashen faced? Did he take the news in deadly quiet, or did he scream and cry?

And what of the immortal horses? They've lost two companions today, mortal Pedasos, the golden horse, and Patroclus, the only human, it's said, who could ever control them. How do immortal horses grieve? Will they continue to serve Achilles, or will they gallop back to the heavenly meadows that they came from? Patroclus had a girl whom he was fond of, a war captive. She could have expected to travel back to Phthia with him after the war and become his wife; now will she simply be passed on again, a piece of war booty?

The next day, things are quiet, just a few skirmishes. Hector is out with his men, and I find myself once more in Andromache's chamber. I don't quite know how it's happened, but I seem now to have found myself a role as the little King of the City's nursemaid. I don't sing or make those silly noises to him that some women do, but he stays calm and quiet when I've got him. Andromache hasn't made a conscious decision to let me take him, I think, but she has other things on her mind at the moment, and doesn't have the time or the energy to worry about her son as long as he's quiet and happy.

Not everyone else is happy, of course. Some of Andromache's slaves are resentful of me, and the way I've suddenly stepped in among them. They used to pet him and make such a fuss of him when his parents were around, I think they believe that one of them should be his nursemaid while his usual one recovers. (Mind, they were never so attentive when Hector or Andromache weren't there, of course.) There's one woman called Khepa, who's especially jealous of me. Sometimes, as she comes past, she jabs the little king with a bronze pin, to make him cry, so it seems that he's upset with me.

So far, her tactics haven't worked, and I'm still in charge of Astyanax. This suits me, of course. I'm getting quite fond of the little boy, though there is still something about him that makes my heart tighten up, I don't know why. I'm not letting myself get too attached to him, just in case.

But as a slave without a job at the moment, I have to look after myself, or I'll end up as one of the laundry slaves, scrubbing clothes in the cold and dirty river until my hands turn raw and red. For the moment, I'll just try to make myself quietly indispensable wherever I can.

How I used to resent being Cassandra's slave, and how I wish now I still was! It breaks my heart to think of her still shut up in her room like a common prisoner, or a mad woman. I'm not even allowed back in the little cupboard of a room where I used to sleep. That means that now I have to find myself another sleeping place; and no one bothers to make that easy for slaves. One or two of Andromache's slaves will sleep on the floor outside her chamber, others must find places where they can. The kitchen slaves have a shed in a small yard at the back, the indoor slaves bed down wherever there's a space that isn't in someone else's way. There's a sloping place under the eaves where most of the women slaves huddle down together. It gets unbearably hot sometimes and flies also like it, but everyone's together, and that protects you from any drunken men who might be on the rampage looking for an available girl.

Andromache's slaves are gleeful that I've ended up here; there was bad feeling that I used to have what they called a 'room' of my own. It was hardly a room, that little cupboard, but it seemed so to them.

I feel as though I've got off on the wrong foot with everyone now – I didn't think I used to give myself airs, but now they're saying I did, and they're enjoying what they see as my downfall. I wonder if I've left it too late to make allies among Andromache's slaves.

There are so many things I have to think about now, it's hurting my head. And always at the back of my mind this feeling of dread. The feeling that soon there are going to be greater things to worry about than where I'm going to sleep.

Not much news is reaching us now from the Greek camps. We find out however, why Patroclus was wearing his friend's armour – it seemed that he was so upset about the carnage being inflicted upon the Greeks, and by their despondency in the face of Hector's assault, he persuaded Achilles to let him ride out before them, wearing his armour, just to inspire them, and discourage the Greeks.

Perhaps that appealed to Achilles's pride – that even

the sight of someone who looked like him would strike terror into the enemy, even though he was still sticking to his own resolve not to fight. But Achilles made Patroclus promise that on no account would he actually go into battle, or try to get near the walls of Troy. Too much pride again – from Patroclus, this time. I suppose he thought he was doing so well that nothing could stop him, and the gods would lead him through the gates of Troy in triumph. How wrong it is for men to take the support of the gods for granted. The gods can forgive us many things, but they never forgive us for excessive pride.

This evening all the triumph is in the Trojan camp. Hector isn't in the citadel tonight; instead, he's holding a great banquet under the stars so all his men can celebrate the day's successes and think about those to come.

Chapter Twenty-four

I had the dream again. I haven't had it for a long time, but now it's even more vivid than ever. The flames rising into a black night sky. Battlements, towers, all bursting into terrible, brilliant flame-flowers. Sometimes I see it from land, this time I'm in a little boat. Dark-haired sailors staring out by the swaying light of a single lantern. The creaking and cracking of wood and sails. No one rowing, just letting the wind take us.

And on the far horizon, that sudden rim of flame....

I wake up drenched in sweat, sitting bolt upright. I think I may have screamed out. The women on either side of me wake up too and grumble at me for waking them.

I don't know what time it is. It's still dark, and stiflingly hot beneath the sloping roof. I don't dare go back to sleep, and so I lie there, until the grey light of dawn starts to sift through the shutters.

It seems that no one quite knows where Hector is, or what his plans are. Andromache starts one thing then another, calls to one slave then changes her mind, picks up her weaving then drops it, and shouts at everyone. All her tensions have come to a head, and no one can say or do anything right. Her usual calm dignity has quite deserted her this morning. I think we all understand her anxiety, and for once this morning, everyone's working together to try and keep her happy.

Then the news comes in that Hector is in the city, by the Scaean Gate, and he's calling for her. Quick as a flash, she jumps to her feet, flings a scarf over her hair, and gestures to the nearest slave to pick up Astyanax from the blanket where he's been crawling. The nearest slave happens to be myself.

We hurry through the palace, through the courtyard, down the main road of the citadel. Everything is busy this morning, rushing slaves carrying things, collecting bread from the baker's, carts delivering great flasks of wine or spring water, fighting men saying goodbye to their wives or children, windows being flung open and women calling to their neighbours. Andromache passes through the mêlée almost unnoticed, but at the Scaean Gate, someone recognises her and directs her up the steps to the top of the high watchtower, where Hector is.

He's in full glorious battle armour, Achilles's god-given armour, his helmet on his head, his great shield and spear stacked against the battlement wall. As he sees his wife, his face breaks into a smile beneath the blue-plumed helmet, he takes her in his arms and hugs her in an awkward metallic embrace.

Andromache doesn't smile, and he has to wipe away her tears. 'Don't fret, my darling,' he says. 'Not when things are going so well for us.'

'I can't help it. I just feel that this can't last.'

'Nonsense. The gods are with us. Today will be a turning point, just you wait and see.'

'But suppose the Greeks get as far as the walls?

Suppose they try to storm that weak spot by the fig tree? Patroclus nearly made it yesterday. Suppose they come back? Shouldn't you be up here protecting us rather than down by the ships?'

'Darling wife, leave the tactics to me. I know what I'm doing. Now let me give my son a big kiss, then I must go off and assemble my men.'

Andromache turns to me and nods to bring the child forward, which I do. But Astyanax hasn't seen this new armour before, and the great glittering helmet hides his father from him. Instead of going into Hector's outstretched arms, he screams in terror and buries his head on my breast.

For a moment, Hector and Andromache look shocked at his reaction, then they realise what's caused it. Hector laughs, takes off the great helmet and lays it carefully on the ground. He runs a hand through his dark curls, which have been flattened by the helmet, his brown eyes are sparkling. He looks as fresh as a man just out of his bath. He reaches out to his son, who this time goes happily into his arms. For a few moments it could be any father with any son, as he nuzzles the little boy, and tosses him into the air. Even Andromache smiles at the sight.

Then finally he hands the boy back to me, and I retreat to the edge of the battlements while he takes his wife by the shoulders and they whisper tenderly to each other. They would make a fine king and queen of Troy, and little Astyanax a handsome crown prince, in a peaceful city, the Greeks long departed, the flax fields blue again and Hector's well-trained horses galloping over the plain. This is the future as it should be.

The rest of the day goes achingly slowly in Andromache's chamber. It's stifling, but she doesn't seem to notice. The door is shut, and her slave women, seven of them and myself, are busy at our looms. Andromache herself is busy on a strip of dark red, which she's been working on for ages. It will have a pattern of black horses on it eventually, and will make a blanket for their great double bed. The little King of the City is playing with his wooden blocks, building towers and knocking them down.

Every minute drags by, every hour, as the sun god crawls slowly over a sky white with heat. From below, we sometimes hear a man shouting, or a horse whinnying, but there's no way of knowing what's going on. Andromache seems determined to keep it that way, as with her head down, she carries on with her weaving, the strip of red becoming noticeably deeper all the time. When the little king starts getting fretful, Khepa and another woman take over and play with him, keeping their voices down all the time. They build towers for him, they play clap-hands and peek-a-boo, they let him stand up against their chairs, and urge him to take a step. On another day, we'd take him to his grandparents' rooms and let him play happily there and be spoiled with almond cakes and sips of watered wine, but today, I don't think he'd be welcome. Eventually, he falls asleep in Khepa's arms, and she can't resist shooting a triumphant glance or two in my direction.

We don't eat, and the heat builds up. It must be well into the afternoon by now. The women are flushed and hair sticks to their cheeks. I can feel the sweat running down inside my robe. Still Andromache sits, stone-faced, her shuttle passing to and fro, in a kind of trance.

One of the women seems about to pass out from the heat. We've drunk all the water in the chamber, and I think we need some more. I go over to Andromache, lean over her and whisper that we need water – may I go and fetch some? She comes briefly out of her trance. 'Go on. If you must.'

Leaving Andromache's still and stifling chamber, I suddenly burst out into the stone-cool of the corridor, and a welcome half-darkness. Coolness runs over me like a river – it's almost like a draught of fresh water.

But it's not calm out here. People are rushing about here and there, going to the ramparts, coming from the ramparts, muttering half-stories to each other that I can't hear. Selfishly I forget about the water and my poor thirsty companions and make my own way up there.

And I wish I hadn't.

Chapter Twenty-five

The King is there, and he looks at a sight which no father should have to see. The battlements are full of people, but they have cleared a space around him and the Queen. The Queen is weeping silently, the old King is tearing his grey hair. He is literally tearing it. It comes away in white wisps in his fists. It must be hurting him, but he doesn't notice.

And then I look over someone's shoulder, and down on the plain below, I too see the sight which is causing so much horror.

For a while I can't talk or say anything. I can't look at it for very long, and I creep back from the battlements, and towards the stairs. I meet a man – I know him by sight – he waits on the tables during royal feasts – a plump, kind man. He's leaning back against the wall, shaking with horror. He's seen it all, and soon he starts to tell the story to me and some more slaves who haven't been there to witness it.

For today has been the day of Achilles's revenge. He came swooping down like a great eagle into the ranks of the Greeks and Trojans, wearing new and glittering armour. His charioteer, Automedon, brought him into the ranks, the immortal horses galloping for their lives. He fought first from his chariot and then on foot, and everywhere men were falling like flies before him. 'I swear to you, it was a god killing those people,' whispers my plump little friend. 'Not a man.'

The Trojan army had been divided into two. Hector was still down at the camp, unaware for some time that his great enemy had emerged from his long silence among the Myrmidon tents. The other part of the army had been scattered around the walls – maybe Hector had taken to heart Andromache's warning about the weak point in the defences and confronted with this gleaming, glittering destroyer, many men stormed back through the great gates, closing them behind them, perhaps hoping to rain missiles down upon Achilles from the ramparts, since he was unstoppable on the ground.

The message reached Hector at about noon, and soon he came back across the plain. He drew nearer and nearer the city in his chariot. And Achilles paused in his murderous spree to watch his approach. At the gate of the lower city, Hector came to a halt and descended from his chariot. Achilles waited for him, a hundred yards away, still as a silver statue, holding his great spear.

All around them, everything went quiet. Men shrunk away, and away, so that the great armies were almost unnoticed before the two men, facing each other across the dust. What a strange sight it must have made – Hector, in Achilles's wonderful armour, the armour he had stripped from Patroclus's body only the day before, and Achilles in new armour – where had he found it? – equally wonderful, equally glittering, with a great embossed shield, covered, so men say, who caught a glimpse of it, with peaceful, happy scenes of everyday life, though now stained and marked with blood from the men Achilles had already killed.

Did Hector see his death waiting for him? For as Achilles started to advance, slowly and deliberately, Hector did the last thing you would ever have imagined of him – he turned and ran.

Here my friend had picked up the story from half a dozen men who'd witnessed it. But there was no doubt that Hector, clad in his heavy armour and clutching his great spear, ran and ran, around the city walls. And also armoured, also stepping lightly and effortlessly, sprinted his fate – Achilles. Already they're exaggerating how far Hector ran – three times around the walls, someone is saying, though I can't believe that.

Hector ran as far as the washing pools by the river – and there, suddenly gaining his courage, he stopped, turned round, and faced his pursuer.

People say that for most of the time, Achilles is gentle and courteous, that you couldn't want for a more considerate or kinder host – he's not a great thug like Agamemnon or Menelaus. That he doesn't enjoy killing for its own sake and will only do it to avenge an insult. They say that he can play the lyre as well as any poet, and that he learned healing skills from his old tutor, Cheiron the centaur, and that many men go to him with unhealable wounds for him to treat.

They say all that. But they say that in a rage, the red fury descends in front of his eyes, and he's merciless and unstoppable until his blood-lust has been glutted and he's had his revenge. Against any other man Hector could have stood his ground and indeed, now he'd decided to fight, he fought bravely and skilfully.

At one point in the fighting, he put all his weight into

launching his spear at Achilles. The spear rammed into the great shield, hovered there vibrating for a few seconds, then fell shivering to the ground. Achilles pushed it aside with his foot, and then lurched at a now defenceless Hector.

Achilles knew the weak points in his own armour. He plunged the spear through a gap in the neck-plate, and rammed it hard home, tearing flesh and sinew and bone.

The Greeks who'd been hanging back now came slowly forward, peering in fascination at the dying man writhing on the ground. Apparently with his last breath, Hector begged that he be given a proper burial and not merely thrown to the dogs, and he lived just long enough to hear Achilles's contemptuous retort.

Chapter Twenty-six

Can anything be worse than death?

Yet what I witnessed just now from the battlements was worse, much worse. What Priam and Hecuba were seeing from the battlements was the desecration of the body of their dear son.

And what I saw being dragged behind the wheels of Achilles's great chariot wasn't Hector, not the tall smiling hero, with his sparkling brown eyes and his dark curls, who only a few hours ago was standing on the battlements in all his power. This was a dust-and-blood bespattered rag, a limp piece of detritus, like something chucked out of a slaughterhouse or abandoned after a flood. Something not even fit for the dogs. This *thing* being dragged in the dust round the city wasn't Hector.

I stumble down the stairs and into the corridor, where I bump into two of Andromache's women. Their faces are intent and busy with the task Andromache has just given them. 'We have to fetch hot water so he can have a bath when he gets back,' says one. 'Come on, you can help.'

I can't say anything. I just sag against the wall and shake my head weakly. They see what my meaning must be, and their eyes widen with shock. 'Oh no!' says one. 'It can't be!'

'It is,' I say.

'Will you tell *her*?'

'I…I can't,' I say. How can I be the one who brings those words to her?

The women stare at me, hands to their mouths in horror. They aren't going to tell her, either. The corridor is filling with people now, silent, streaming people, who *know*. While Andromache is preparing a bath for her returning hero…

I don't tell her. We don't have to. For now comes a great keening wave of sorrow from the women on the roof. It penetrates the corridor below, and at last must have found its way through the door of Andromache's room, for suddenly the door is flung open, and there she stands.

For a moment she looks around her hopefully as though the news might be something else, some other sorrow that's nothing to do with her. But then she sees the look on everyone's faces – and then she too *knows*.

Heavens help me, I'm not the one who goes to Andromache in her hour of need. Two of her women, who've been with her for years, run to her, and lift her up before she falls. It takes a long time before she utters a sound, her head lolling like a doll's, hair escaping from its bronze pins, hands waving wildly.

And then she too screams and her screams merge into one great scream that seems to resonate throughout the entire palace, going from room to room to room, up staircases, along corridors, a fearful single long drawn-out cry of anguish.

Priam's palace is now nothing but a house of sorrow. Sorrow is in the air, creeps through the walls, insinuates its way under closed doors, blows through windows like a poisonous mist. Andromache, Hecuba, Priam, all terrible in their bereavement. And strangely, it brings everyone in the house of Priam together, slaves and free, as though we're all now part of the same family.

It's the slaves now who are holding everything together, slaves who are organising the household routines, telling kings and princes what they should do, where they should go, urging them to rest, or drink or eat; and the royal ones who obey meekly.

These days have aged Priam by twenty years – suddenly he's become a little old man, frail, vulnerable, quavering. Hecuba is drowned with grief in her room, Andromache is pale and dazed. We're all expecting Hector to walk in at any minute, his big, safe comforting presence, his certainty, his ability to restore order. He'll set things to rights, we all feel. No one can quite grasp the huge fact of his absence.

It's left to Deiphobus, who now more than ever seems like a failed recreation of Hector, edgy where Hector was confident, unbending where Hector was firm, putting people's backs up where Hector instilled confidence, to try keep everything working. And Helenus, grave and austere, who knows the gods, but finds it hard to talk to men. Paris is trying hard to do and say the right things, but now even more than ever, the unspoken feeling that this is all *his* fault makes it hard for him to take authority.

The day of Hector's death produced more horrors that on another occasion would have wiped everything else out, for among the men that Achilles killed was Troilus, laughing fair-haired Troilus, scarcely a man, and still, as far as his mother was concerned, the baby boy-child of the family. I think she's taken his death almost harder than

Hector's. And two more of Priam's sons also fell that day.

What will happen now to the house of Priam? Only Deiphobus, Helenus and Paris remain of the legitimate sons. Andromache is starting to realise the pathos of her position. No longer is she the chief wife of the palace, next to the Queen, she's now just another lost woman. And her little son, once revered as the future King of Troy is just another surplus mouth to feed. He's never going to become king now – someone else will take over the succession and it will be that person's sons who will succeed him. Even Astyanax's life isn't secure now – for it's in the way of things that a new king might kill off any rivals – even small children – who are in his way. Looking at Priam's frailty now, it seems that day won't be far away. Poor Andromache. Poor little King of the City.

But as far as Priam is concerned now, the worst thing is not being able to bury Hector. Hector lies somewhere in the dust near Achilles's camp – and no one knows what fate Achilles has in mind for his body, except that it seems that relentless Achilles is pursuing his enmity beyond death. Without the proper funeral rites, Hector's spirit can never rest, can never go to the land of heroes; and his family's grief will be a raw wound that can never heal.

Everything is silent now on the dusty plain – we hear that Achilles is planning elaborate funeral games for his beloved Patroclus – and piling horror on horror, among the gifts he intends to give his dead friend are the souls of several young Trojan men, whom he took to be ransomed – but whose families will see them no more. You can hardly believe there is anything mortal about this man, so implacable is his rage.

Priam wanders about the palace like an old tramp, unkempt, his garments torn, his face smeared with dust and dirt. Days pass, each another day that Hector lies unburied somewhere in Achilles's camp. His remaining sons and daughters try to comfort him, but he only gets angry, and thrusts them aside. Citizens clamour at the gates of the palace, wanting only to pay their respects and give him their sympathies, but he won't listen to them, either. We worry that he's going mad.

One consolation for me is that everyone's too busy to stop me from going into Cassandra's room. She's quiet now; it seems for the moment the god is leaving her alone. But she's too frightened to leave her chamber now, in case he possesses her again before her parents. We sit on her bed, spinning flax to pass the hours, and we talk about the time we've spent together over the years. We never knew that we were friends then, but now it seems that we were, after all.

Chapter Twenty-seven

Priam has a plan, and it's one that casts fear into the hearts of everyone who hears it. He announces it one morning in the great hall. He's combed his hair and washed his face, and now seems more like his old self. His plan is this – if Achilles won't return Hector's body to him, then he will go and ask Achilles for it.

There's a gasp of horror as he outlines this, but since there's no Hector to dissuade him from doing it, the plan develops over the morning. He'll take his chariot, and a mule cart full of Trojan treasure – he isn't so naïve as to think Achilles will let him have the body back for nothing.

And then suddenly I'm part of it.

'How can you possibly ask Achilles all that?' says Deiphobus. 'You only know a few words of Greek. Let me come with you. I can talk to him for you.

'What? Certainly not. He'd kill us both.

'You must take someone, someone who'll speak for you.'

'Who? Can't take any of Hector's spies. He'd kill us for sure then.'

'Someone who speaks Greek. Someone who isn't a threat...' This is one of Priam's sons from outside the palace, Melias. I never knew he was aware of me, but suddenly he's turning to me, and everyone else in the great hall turns to look. 'Take that Greek slave,' he says. 'She'll interpret for you, and she won't be a threat to anyone.' And if she gets killed, he's thinking, but not saying, nobody'll mind…

Priam is determined. Hecuba pleads with him to think again, but he won't. The next thing is to make his chariot ready, and a mule cart to carry the treasures with which he wants to ransom his son. In the courtyard we hear the clatter of wheels and hooves. Then there's the matter of the ransom. If the King wants Achilles to release his son, the ransom must be a splendid one – a *king's* ransom. A group of slaves goes with the King to his treasury and soon they're carrying it all into the great hall. They say the treasures of Troy are not what they were before this war – but what is brought up seems pretty splendid to me; there's a pile of great brocaded robes, of the rich and glimmering fabric that comes from the far ends of the earth, twelve cloaks of softest, warmest wool, as light as thistledown, piles of blankets, of white linen tunics. Then heavy gold bars, bronze tripods and cauldrons, and lastly an embossed and patterned golden cup, one of the King's most precious possessions, that he'd brought back long ago from a mission to Thracia.

Then, as the mule cart and its driver, a bewildered middle-aged man called Ideus, wait in the courtyard, they find a sort of wicker cradle, which they fix in the cart; this will carry the pile of treasure safely, and, though no one is daring to say it, will also hold a body securely.

I watch all this happen, still not believing that I am to be sent along too. The afternoon wears on – it will be dark soon. And then finally all is ready. The King climbs into his chariot – old though he is, he can still control horses; Ideus climbs into the driver's seat of the mule cart. Someone fetches a grey shawl to cover me, and I too, am hoisted up on to the mule cart. We're ready to leave.

It's late now. Soon the sun will be setting, but the sky is overcast, so it will be a colourless sunset; perhaps even the sun god knows this is a sombre and solemn occasion.

Priam's chariot rattles through the courtyard gates, and down the paved road. Our heavy mule cart rattles even more loudly behind it. We go through the upper citadel, the Scaean Gate, the last place where I saw Hector alive, through the lower city and the city gates. I know that all the citizens of Troy are there to watch us go, but in deference to the grief of their King, they have hidden themselves, in doorways, behind pillars, in windows, on rooftops. We feel the combined sadness of hundreds of people, holding their breaths, still as statues, as we ride by.

Then through the gates, out into the plain, and a sweep down the old wagon road to the harbour. The Greek camp is barely a mile away, and Achilles is encamped perhaps a mile beyond that – a walk that would take a young man no time at all, but for us it will be a slow and dangerous ride. The mule driver beside me tut-tuts and clicks his teeth – he doesn't want to be doing this; he fears the Greeks are going to slaughter us as we ride by in our mule cart laden with treasure. It's a hazardous venture all round – but King Priam is beyond caring. He stands upright in his chariot ahead of us, tall and straight again – he has a purpose and it has made him briefly young once more.

The sky grows dingy with the approach of night, and the great plain leading down to the sea is grey as the sea

142

itself. Everywhere there are signs of battle – the ground churned up and trampled, bits of detritus lying about everywhere, smashed chariots, broken spear hafts, shreds of leather armour. All the human bodies have been taken away, but there are dead horses, with clouds of flies around them. And everywhere the light sandy soil is stained with dark pools that must be blood. Seagulls swoop and cry overhead, looking for food.

The high walls of Troy with the flaming torches around the battlements are growing more and more distant. Now we couldn't hear someone calling to us from there. Darkness collects around us. Ideus has lit a couple of lanterns and hung them from the sides of the cart.

Before we can get to the Greek camp we come to the place where the river Scamander washes across the plain in a shallow ford. The mule gets it into its head that this is the place to stop for a drink, and the driver can't dissuade it. They don't say stubborn as a mule for nothing. This gives Priam's horses the same idea. So we all get down, the King from his chariot, Ideus and myself from the mule cart, and there we stand, listening to the slurp of the animals and the creak and rattle of the cart and chariot. Perhaps it's the ilex trees surrounding us, but it seems to have got very dark all at once. There are little rustlings all around us. For a moment I think I see a little owl sitting on a branch, staring hard at me, its feathers glimmering.

And though there's no lantern on the King's chariot and no moon in the sky, there suddenly seems to be enough light to drive by, a strange, silvery light. I feel odd, remote, detached from myself. This is the strangest journey I have even been on, and now I'm not afraid. I don't think the King is either.

We ford the river here. Then we follow the old wagon road, which used to go down to the harbour so that wagons laden with all the things they used to love in Troy, ivory, decorated pots, spices, perfumed oils, could trundle back to the citadel. It's not been used for such cargoes for a long time, but the road is still clear, and the silvery light washes down it to show us the way, as though we're being guided.

And now we can see the glitter of the sea, and massed all over the plain, the beached Greek ships, hundreds and hundreds of them. I'd often wished to see what the Greek camp looked like, but never dreamed that I would.

We can smell the Greek camp before we approach it, smoke and rotting garbage and sewage, almost drowning the clear salty tang of the sea. Watch-fires gleam through the dark mass of the camp, but all is strangely silent.

And then we pass the main gate, and see guards sprawled in sleep. They shouldn't be asleep like this. Again, I have this strange feeling that someone is making sure we are led safely through.

We trundle slowly over the road that runs between the camp and the great boats, a wide clear road that once would have been lined with old trees, but now there's nothing there, except great black hulks, rearing up like walls around us.

Then a broad empty space. And finally we come to another gate, built strongly of planks, set into a wavy fence of palings, and beyond that pinpoints of light. The camp of Achilles.

Chapter Twenty-eight

After the noise and clanking of the cart and chariot, silence falls very suddenly and deeply around us. The gate swings slowly open, all by itself. I scramble down from the mule cart and go to help the King. He steps down slowly and carefully from his chariot, an old man once more. Then Ideus the mule driver is there too. He doesn't say anything, but he's shaking his head fearfully. We look through the gates, and see the black shapes of tents, and beyond, a rectangular, plank-built building.

For just a few seconds, all three of us are standing there, taking it in our various ways. Ideus is silent and grumpy, I'm oddly excited, but frightened too. And the King – the gods only know what the King can be thinking, knowing he's now so close to the body of his beloved son. He shakes his head and is silent for a while. He's not going to share his thoughts with a slave girl and a mule driver. 'Come,' he says eventually. 'Lead the horses through.'

And he steps into the approach to Achilles's camphouse, a single, frail figure with white hair.

I've never handled great chariot horses like these before, but I take the reins and they follow me meekly enough. Inside the camp, I tether the reins to a post, and I guess Ideus does the same with the mule cart.

Priam is standing before the half open door of

Achilles's lodge. Light comes through and a rumble of voices. He takes a deep breath. Before we go in, he turns to me. 'You will tell him everything I say,' he says. 'And you will tell me what he says in return. Everything.'

The mule driver waits outside. King Priam and I go through the door into the brightly lit hall.

They've fixed up a splendid lodging for Achilles here. The plank walls are hung with bright blankets, lamps glow from ornate bronze tripods, there are chests, carved chairs and a great table, spread with silver bowls and painted pots, perhaps booty from cities Achilles has sacked. A number of men – and a couple of women – stare at us from the shadows. A serving man holds a great pitcher of wine.

And at the table, a man sits alone.

There's a carved chair next to him, an empty chair. Perhaps this is where Patroclus used to sit. The man is eating, all by himself. Roast meat and bread litters the table. He doesn't seem to have eaten very much, but there's a silver cup halfway to his lips. He puts it down, and stares at us.

He's as they described him, though it's always different to meet someone in real life, no matter what you've heard of them. I see broad shoulders, a stocky build. The arm holding the cup is tanned walnut-dark, muscular. His hair is an unruly mass of tight golden curls, bleached by the sun, and he wears gold earrings, like a sailor. He's not handsome, like Hector – they were right about that – a bruiser's nose, that looks as through it's been in some fights, half-closed eyes that show a chip of bright emerald iris. But it's a face that compels you to look at it. I imagine he'd have a nice smile, though he's not smiling now.

He doesn't speak. No one speaks.

Then in a clear, tense voice, the King says, 'Achilles, I have come to talk to you. This slave will translate what I say.'

Which I try to do, into my best Greek, which suddenly feels rusty. Everyone's looking at me now.

And then the old King rushes forward and falls to his knees in front of the other man. He takes the strong hand, the hand which has just put down the cup, and kisses it almost like a lover. 'You have a father too, Achilles,' he says brokenly. 'Suppose it was *your* body lying torn and desecrated on the ground. Wouldn't *he* be pleading with his son's killer to let it go, to be given a proper burial rather than being left for the dogs?'

Tentatively I come forward, and start to try and translate these terrible words, but Achilles looks up sharply at me and waves me to be silent. 'I understand you,' he says to the King.

'You have killed so many of my sons, you and your fellows,' says the old King. 'Don't you feel any compassion? Doesn't it make you ashamed to see me kneeling here, kissing the hand of their murderer?'

And to my surprise, I see that at these words Achilles's eyes also fill with tears. They gather in his green eyes, sparkling in the lamplight, and start to run down his cheeks. I find that I have a lump in my throat too.

In the silence of the hut men shift and cough nervously. A pretty woman extracts herself from the shadows, comes forward, with little tiny steps, and then retreats again. I wonder if this is Briseis, the famous Briseis who caused all this. She's small, slight and fair-haired, with a sad little wide-eyed face, someone who's seen much she'd rather not have seen.

For a long time, nothing is said, just the strange sound of men crying. Men don't like to cry in public, I know that.

Then finally Achilles gives a deep shuddering sigh, pushes back his chair, and puts his arm on the old man's shoulders. He looks across the room at me. 'Tell the King what I say,' he says in Greek. He speaks slowly, deliberately, swallowing down his sobs. As he speaks, I try to translate his words.

'Noble King Priam, I know how hard it must have been for you to come here. And yes, you remind me of my own father. He's grey-haired now, though he was strong as a lion. He has courage, like you. I'm sorry for what you've endured. I can't...I wouldn't...undo what I've done. But it's done now. Hector, Patroclus, they're both dead. The dead don't come back. Sit by my side, in Patroclus's empty chair. Sit with me and drink some wine. We'll drink together.'

But Priam scrambled to his feet. 'I'll kneel to you, Achilles, but I won't drink with you. Look, outside in my chariot, I've brought treasures. Piles of treasures. Gold and silks and bronze, all the stuff you want. In return I want only my son's body back, noble Achilles.'

I see Achilles's face suddenly grow dark; it's a glimpse of the terrible anger that drove him round the walls of Troy. 'You're going too far now, old man, talking about treasure. If I give you back your son's body, it's because *I've* decided to do it. Translate that!'

I do, softening the anger a little. Then Achilles goes on, 'The old man mustn't see Hector's body in the state it's in. *Don't,*' he snaps at me, 'translate that! Just tell him to bring in the treasure he's got to show me. You, Briseis, go and clean up the body. Take some men with you. *You* help her, Greek slave; it isn't a job for a lady.'

'He wants to see the treasure, Sire,' I gabble to the King. I hope he hasn't understood what Achilles said about the body. 'Can Ideus bring it in, Sire?'

The little soft-faced woman beckons to me. 'Come,' she says. Her voice is as soft as her face. We leave the hut while Priam is arranging about the treasure.

We step into the darkness of the camp. Men sitting at the mouths of their tents watch us curiously. We're going round the back where the stables are. I smell straw and manure, and hear horses neighing. She stops, and puts a light hand on my arm.

'Don't be shocked,' she says, in that little voice. 'The body's here.'

There's a pile of something by the manure heap. I recognise what it is, and I almost gag, ramming my hand into my mouth. Two of Achilles's men are standing beside us with a torch. I wish the torch wasn't there so I didn't have to see it.

Hector's naked body is pale and livid, marked with scratches that I can see, and probably terrible wounds that I can't. Yet, in spite of several days left lying in the heat, I can smell no corruption. But his jaw is slack and his eyes are open and glazed.

Briseis waves to the men to take the body to a tent. 'My lord's bath tent,' she says. 'We'll clean him up there.'

I'm glad she says *we* – I've never cleaned a dead body before and the thought of having to do it on my own was filling me with dread.

The men take the body into the tent and lay it down on a blanket on the ground. Then they back out, respectfully, and wait outside. There's already a big terracotta bowl full of water there. Briseis looks at me. 'You're too young to be doing this. I've done it before.'

She wrings out a linen cloth, and slowly, carefully, starts to clean Hector's cold face, moving down the body, rinsing out the cloth several times as she goes. 'Every day,' she says, softly, 'he's been dragging it round Patroclus's funeral pyre. And every night, though he doesn't know, I've been doing this.' She gets to her feet, and making sure that no one else sees, goes to a little carved wooden cabinet, and takes out a pottery flask. She removes the stopper and hands it to me to smell. A strong, herby fragrance comes from it.

'His divine mother, Thetis, gave me this one day. I hope I never have to do what she asked me with it, but it's very strong, goes a long way. There's enough for more than one man here.'

She sighs. 'I love my lord. I'd go to the ends of the earth for him, but he can be cruel. Hector was a good man, one of our people. I can't let his body rot in front of us.' She dribbles a few drops of the pungent liquid on to Hector's chest and rubs it over his body. The scent fills the tent.

When she's finished, she takes a big bolt of clean white linen cloth from a chest. She shows me what to do, and together we wind it round and round Hector's body. The body feels limp and clammy. I hope I never have to do this again; but I've got over my feeling of wanting to be sick – this is just a task to be done. She ties a cloth around his slack jaw, and closes his eyes. Then she lays a blanket – a fine one, woven of blue wool, with yellow stripes and a fringe – on the floor, and together we lift the body on to it. She wraps it snugly round him, as someone wraps a cloak around themselves in icy weather, tightly round his face, pinned in placc on his breast, so the bandage round his jaw is hidden. Then with her fingers she teases the still-vibrant brown curls over his forehead so his face is framed by them. Now the body doesn't look so terrible.

'There,' she says. 'Now his father can see him. And my lord will never know what I've been doing – if you don't tell a man something, he won't ask. That's the way they are.'

At first I found her little voice and delicate footsteps irritating, but I see now that there are different ways for people to have courage, and that there's a lot of calm courage in Briseis. She saw her husband and family killed by this man whom she now has come to love, but she is also doing what she thinks is right. I hope she didn't have too bad a time at the hands of that horrible old Agamemnon.

There's a rumour that Achilles's fate is somehow tied up with that of Hector – that his dcath will follow Hector's. But I wonder how this can happen – his immortal mother Thetis dipped him in the river Styx, so that he wouldn't be vulnerable to death, or so it's said.

And yet Thetis has given Briseis this ointment which has at least kept Hector's mortal body from corrupting. I wish she could have brought him back from the dead, but not even the gods can do that.

Briseis summons the two men who helped us earlier and together they carry Hector's body from the tent. I show them where to lay it in the cradle in the mule cart.

Now his father must be told.

Chapter Twenty-nine

All is quiet in Achilles's lodge, the lamps burning low, no music, men talking in whispers. At the great table sit Achilles and Priam. Priam stares ahead of him, fingers drumming the table. He sits in Patroclus's chair and I see Achilles looking at him from the corners of his eyes. He must be remembering nights that he and Patroclus sat there together, lamps burning low, wine down to the lees, laughing and planning and going over the day's events, while their women waited patiently for them behind the curtained-off sleeping chambers. Poor Briseis – she may have had Achilles's heart, but only Patroclus had his soul. I hope it's never my lot to love a man like Achilles.

I go up to the two men and say softly, 'My lords, we have finished. The...' Oh, I was going to say 'body', but I can't, 'Hector', but I can't, 'your son', but I can't say that either.

But the meaning is clear enough. Priam pushes back his chair roughly. 'I will see my son,' he says. Achilles gets up too, and tries to restrain him, no doubt imagining the condition he thinks the corpse must be in by now, but the old King pushes him aside.

No one follows him out. He stays outside for a long time, and when he stumbles into the hall again, his hair looks wispy and his eyes are wild.

He comes back to Patroclus's seat at the table, sits down, and stares ahead into nothingness. After a long while, Achilles says, gently, like a courteous host, 'Will you have something to eat and drink, old man? I don't suppose you've tasted food for days.'

Priam shakes his head, but when Achilles pushes a cup of wine towards him, he drinks it. He tastes a little bread too, and Achilles pretends to join him. This will be good for the King, I know – he's fasted since Hector was killed.

The wine relaxes Priam a little, though his eyes still have a wild look. I can see that he's working something out, and soon he says it. I'm on hand to translate, of course. 'I must bury my son decently, Achilles. You know that.'

Achilles isn't going to deny Priam this, I'm glad to say. 'How long will you need?'

Priam stares at Achilles, firmly now. 'I want twelve days,' he says. 'We must build a funeral pyre and you people have taken all our wood. We must have a feast, and we must bury his bones properly. Twelve days.'

'You shall have it. You have my word that none of us – and none of Agamemnon's men – will renew the war for twelve days. Bury your son and may his spirit go in peace.'

Priam just nods in assent. He doesn't thank Achilles – why should he? Then he says, 'I'm tired now. It's too late to go back to my city – I will sleep here, if you'll let me.'

It must be getting towards midnight, by now. Achilles gives orders and a tent is prepared. 'You'll be safe in my camp, but outside my hall in one of my tents,' he says. 'You're not at risk from any of my men, but in case one of Agamemnon's men happens to turn up...'

I wonder what's going to happen to me and Ideus – I don't fancy sharing a sleeping space with the mule driver. But Achilles thinks of that too. I have a tent all to myself – the men who should have slept there must have doubled up with another comrade.

I don't think I'm going to sleep, but I fall off, into dreamless darkness.

But I don't sleep for long. For suddenly I'm being shaken roughly by the shoulders. It's the King's voice I hear. 'Come on, girl,' he says. 'We're not staying here.'

What's happened? The King won't say, not at first. I stumble out into the darkness, and see that Ideus has already untethered the mule, and the King's chariot is waiting as we left it. It's very dark, though, and all I can hear is the fussiness in the King's voice. We have to go! We have to go now!

Ideus unbars the gate of Achilles's camp in the darkness. There are no guards there and oddly, no one seems to be waking up. But I think I catch a glimpse of pale, silvery wings in the darkness, and round, staring eyes.

I'm to ride in the chariot with the King this time. He doesn't want too many people close to the body of his son. We set off, in darkness, but once again, a faint path of light seems to show us the way.

All around us are sleeping enemies, hundreds, thousands of them. The chariot rumbles through the darkness, the mule cart rattles behind. The King doesn't say anything to me, until we get to the gates of the Greek camp. There we see the sleeping guards, still in a dark heap.

'Look at that!' he says in a low voice. 'Sleeping on duty! I'd have them garrotted for that.'

I dare to answer him. 'Someone is protecting you, Sire.'

'The gods sent me a dream. Quite right – I should never have trusted those Greeks.'

'I think you can trust Achilles, Sire.' Strange though it seems, I believe this. I would trust Achilles in anything except his terrible anger.

'One man I can trust, and thousands I can't. I don't intend to end my days as an object of ransom for that old demon, Agamemnon.'

I think he's right, but I don't risk saying any more to him. We rattle on in the darkness, but as we clear the Greek camp, dawn starts to break over the eastern hills, a faint smudge of light in the darkness. Soon we can see the Trojan citadel ahead of us. People must have been waiting for the King, for as soon as we trundle into sight, men come running across the plain to meet us. They run round the horses, asking questions, trying to help, ignoring the awful thing that's resting in the wicker cradle of the mule cart. I get down from the chariot and walk, leaving some of the King's close attendants and guards to comfort him. He chats away to them about our adventure – he seems almost cheerful now.

It's quite light by the time we reach the citadel. But I see a figure standing on the palace battlements. It's Cassandra. As she sees us she screams and screams. I don't know what she's saying, but soon someone comes and leads us away.

But her screams have woken up the entire city. As we arrive at the lower gates, to make our way to the citadel, people have come from their houses, or lean out of their windows, still in night clothes. All around us is moaning, lamenting. Hector has come home.

Chapter Thirty

Without Hector there to see to things, nothing works properly. Preparations for the great funeral feast are causing all sorts of problems. Deiphobus and Helenus are constantly at loggerheads about how things should be done. Neither has that easy authority that we took for granted in Hector. The King stays in his room. Andromache doesn't know what to do with herself – she drifts about the palace finding fault with things. Astyanax is fretful – and the other women won't let me near him – a pity because I was growing quite fond of the little boy. Lady Helen is hardly seen, and Paris is more unpopular than ever.

And Cassandra has been locked away more efficiently now – I can't get in to see her at all. This is Helenus's doing, I think.

With no particular role for me, I'm just doing a good deal of weaving at the moment. I want to keep my head down, just in case someone notices me, and sees that I'm not being much use.

Lady Helen sends for me, though, on the sixth day after Hector's body has been brought home. I find her in her chamber, pale, dressed in grey, dark circles under her eyes, but as beautiful as ever, of course.

'Eirene,' she says. 'I have a task for you but no one must know – do you understand?'

I'm glad that someone wants me for something – but this makes me uneasy, nevertheless.

'Yes, madam.'

'Do you remember Myron, at the Branch of Hyssop? Of course you do. Now, he has something for me there.' She goes to a little box and takes some things out. There's a little clay button, with a mark on it, like a seal impression. And a fine gold and garnet bracelet. Whatever she wants from the little Greek must be costlier than her usual sleeping draught.

She presses the clay tablet into my hand. 'Give him this. It's a message – he'll understand. The gold is an exchange. Hide what he gives you, tell no one and bring it straight back here – do you understand?'

'Yes, madam.'

'There'll be a reward in it for you.'

'Thank you, madam.' But I can't think of any reward that she'll give me that I could want.

I go through the city, to the little dark alley. Shops are closed and work seems to have stopped. Only Hector's funeral is important now, it seems.

The little dark man in the Branch of Hyssop recognises who's sent me. 'What does my lady want today?' he says in Greek. I hand him the little clay tablet. He nods slowly. 'Ah yes. I wondered when she'd be ready for this. And in return…?'

I hold out the gold bracelet. He gives a nasty wolfish grin and takes it from me. Then he disappears into his little back room. He's away a long time. He comes back, holding something in a little cloth, a tiny vial of black glass. He puts it down carefully on a table, wraps it up in the cloth and ties the little bundle tightly up with twine. 'Don't open this,' he says. 'Don't drop it. Hide it on your way home and give it straight to the lady. Don't tell anyone who gave it to you. Understand?'

I understand. Lady Helen is up to something. But it's not my place to know about it. I do as the man says, hide the little bundle in the purse at my belt and hurry back with it to the citadel.

I knock at the Lady Helen's door. When I go in, Paris is standing in the shadows.

'Have you got it, Eirene?'

'Yes, madam.'

But it's Paris who comes forward eagerly and takes the bundle from me. Lady Helen gives me my reward – a little silver chain necklace. I'll never be able to wear it of course – so I shall give it to my goddess, discreetly, or someone will think I've stolen it.

As I leave Lady Helen's room, I hear Paris saying to her, in a low and breathless voice. 'You see? I'll make you proud of me, I promise.'

These twelve days that Achilles has given us to bury Hector in peace are very strange. The Greeks are keeping their word and leaving us alone (though I have a horrible feeling that they might be using this truce to plan their next tactic). We hear fragments of news from the Greek camp – that Achilles still stays quiet among his tents. He plans to return to Phthia, but can't yet bring himself to leave Patroclus's grave. Certainly he isn't much use to the Greeks at the moment; we also hear that Odysseus has sent for Achilles's son Pyrrhus to join his father – perhaps he hopes that Pyrrhus will do what nobody else among the Greeks has been able to do, and get Achilles back fighting again. I wonder what Lady Helen's daughter thinks of this – having to say goodbye to her new young husband, so soon, and seeing him go off to fight against her own mother. Marriage complicates life so – I can't think that I would ever be happy married to someone.

On the plain beyond the citadel, preparations for Hector's funeral continue. A great space has been cleared, and men are bringing wood to make the pyre. They have to go a long way to collect it, these days – it's a slow business. Meanwhile Hector's body lies in the little Temple of Apollo within the citadel walls. I hope Briseis's divine lotion is still keeping him clean and uncorrupted. Every day, Andromache sits by him. She's torn her clothes and dirtied her face – she doesn't look like a noblewoman any more. I can't imagine her grief; she must feel like a ship that has lost its rudder.

But I don't forget my goddess, of course. And on the last day of Hector's lying in state I find an excuse to make my offering to her.

The citadel is empty now – everyone, except for a few guards, has gone down to the plain to look at the great pyre, ready to go. It's higher than two men – the gods only know where they managed to find so much wood. Hector's favourite horse, who's going to be sacrificed, too, waits restlessly, tethered nearby, pawing the ground. He's a fine horse, and I'm sorry that this has to happen – but I suppose that this way, he will get to carry his master into the heroes' land in the afterlife.

The Temple of Pallas near the citadel is empty

– Theano the priestess has gone down to the plain. And I see the great bronze doors are open, and I can peer into the darkness.

I shouldn't go in – but as I stand there, looking in, something seems to draw me in, and I feel sure the goddess won't be angry with me. Is that the sound of beating wings I hear, and are those two round eyes staring at me from a roof beam? That darkness, so secret, so mysterious, pulls me in. I can't resist.

Softly, hearing my footsteps swishing on the cool plaster floor, I go inside. At once, the space closes around me, the strange darkness. I am in a different world. The walls are painted deep red, the ceiling beams are richly carved, a tiny flame burns before the altar. There's a sense of holiness here – everything else is shut out, the noise and bustle of Troy, the war spreading over the plain, the difficulties and anxieties of life. Now there's just cool, numinous darkness, and something more ancient than Troy; something that has been here for more centuries than anyone can remember.

Then I see the strange antique statue of the goddess that has stood here for hundreds, maybe thousands, of years. There's almost nothing more to it now than a straight column of blackened wood – but you can just make out an arm held in the air, as if to hold a spear – but the spear has gone – and a head crowned with a helmet, all not much bigger than a man's forearm. She will inhabit this old statue, use it as a conduit. I am closer to her here than I have ever been.

I fall to my knees before her. 'Holy lady,' I say to her, 'forgive me for coming into your shrine like this.'

There's no voice, but I can feel words forming in my head, as though someone else has spoken them. *Don't worry – all will be well with you...*I can sense the goddess here, though she doesn't reveal herself to me. At once I feel at peace. In spite of everything that has happened and will happen, all will be well. I stay there for a long time, kneeling at her feet, and before I go, I drape Lady Helen's silver necklace over the rough wooden shoulders.

Hector is burned the following day. Huge flames roar and crackle, and the plaintive moaning of all the musicians Troy has to offer goes into the air with them. Andromache's screams are louder than the flames, or the mournful music. Priam is numb with grief, frail as an autumn leaf.

When the flames have died down, the ashes are quenched with wine, and the remains of the great hero are gathered together, wrapped in a gold-edged linen cloth, placed in a chest studded with gold, blue glass and ivory, to be buried beneath a great mound.

...So the Trojans buried Hector, tamer of horses... A poet sings these words at the end of it all, and they hang mournfully in the air.

Chapter Thirty-one

So the truce is over. No one is quite sure what will happen next – how the war will resume. But nobody expects what Paris does now.

The plain lies before us, stretching out towards the sea. Traces of battle – bits of broken armour, chariot wheels, churned up soil – still litter it, but it's silent and empty. No sign of the Greeks. Some Trojans come out and start to practise spear throwing, riding – I think it's all show, just to demonstrate that they're still here.

Then, striding out on to the plain, goes one of the Trojan heralds – one who speaks Greek. He has a message from Paris; he is to go to Achilles. He is to say that all men consider Achilles nothing more than a coward for spending the war sulking in his tent. He is to say that Paris is waiting to fight him – if Achilles is brave enough.

Gods above! Will the herald escape with his life after he's delivered this message? He must be quaking in his boots.

The morning goes by. Nothing happens, apart from the desultory practice. Noon.

Then we hear. Achilles will answer Paris. He is on his way.

For this, everyone in the palace crowds on to the battlements – except the King, of course. He can't bear to watch another son die – as Paris surely must.

Lady Helen isn't there, either. As always, what Lady Helen is doing, or thinking, remains a mystery.

We see the Greeks first, coming in a shimmer like a heat-mirage in the distance. We can't make out who's there at first; we suspect Achilles is there with his Myrmidons. But the word goes out.

And then Paris appears below us on the plain. Everyone draws in a deep breath at the sight of him.

For Paris appears to be dressed for a banquet rather than a fight to the death. He's bare-headed, and his long hair has been curled, gold rings flash in his ears, and his eyes have been outlined in black eye paint. There's probably rouge on his cheeks as well. He's wearing a light silver corselet, which couldn't deflect many blows – more appropriate for games than real fighting. His waist is nipped in tightly with a bronze belt – and he's wearing a bright fringed kilt. He holds no weapons except his little curved bow of hide and ash wood, and a quiver full of arrows at his belt.

We can't understand this. Whatever Paris is, he certainly isn't suicidal. What is he thinking of?

The Greek contingent advances and advances. The shimmer breaks up into an identifiable group of men – and yes, at the centre of it all, walking quickly, is Achilles. He at any rate is in full armour – we can see it glittering as he approaches – the armour in which he killed Hector.

Paris walks forward. We all strain to catch a sight of him. He looks small and slim, like a pretty doll, but he's still close enough for us to hear him speak.

Around him now, other Trojans are gathering, in

some trepidation, I imagine. All are more strongly armed than he – I see some of the very young men – all of whom hate Achilles for the cruel way in which he sacrificed their friends to Patroclus's ghost. Big Aeneas is there, and Glaucus. But they won't interfere – this is Paris's challenge and must be Paris's fight.

The Greeks come closer and closer. I can recognise Achilles in the centre of the group – although his face is concealed by his helmet – by his broad shoulders. He walks with a rolling gait, full of tension and impatience.

Closer and closer. His Myrmidons cluster around him, and behind in the distance, come rank upon rank of the other Greeks. Trojans are gathering too. The air is suddenly clotted and dark with the presence of all of them, fear and anger rising like smoke.

And then at last, the two men face each other. We see Paris from the back, Achilles from the front. Barely the length of three men from each other, Achilles whips off his helmet and hands it to a companion. His curls, brassy in the sunlight, spark up into the air as though fired with life. He leans forward, grasping his great spear in one hand, his ornate shield in the other.

And Paris laughs.

'So good of you to come,' Paris says, his voice light and clear. 'Good of you to rouse yourself. How are you feeling, by the way? Not too tired, I hope?'

Achilles scowls, his face like thunder. He's silent for a long while. Then he lifts up his spear and hurls it to the ground. 'I fight men,' he spits. 'Not painted girls!'

And he spins round, in a great glittering movement, clashing of breastplate and bronze greaves. For a moment, he's there with his back to us all.

And that's the moment Paris seizes.

I knew he was an excellent bowman, but I didn't really understand what that meant until now. In one graceful, elegant gesture, he's whipped an arrow from the quiver, fixed it to his little bow and aimed.

Not straight. Downwards and to the side.

The arrow thrums in the air and catches Achilles, at the back of his leg just above the ankle, where the bronze greaves are tied with leather cords, and where the leg is unprotected. The arrow shivers to a halt in the lower part of Achilles's calf.

But it's only a tiny wound. So small that the hero turns, and pulls it from his own leg and dashes it on to the ground with a snarl of contempt. Then he's off, striding back to the Greek camp.

The Greek soldiers part to let him through. Everyone's bewildered, uncertain, looking first at Paris, then at the departing back of Achilles.

Paris seems quite unworried; in fact he's throwing back his head in what seems almost like triumph.

Achilles strides off, just a faint trickle of blood running down his leg and his boot. His men are going with him now – they're all retreating.

He walks and walks, getting smaller now. Now he's just a few inches high in our sights. The great plain seems to quiver beneath him, the sunlight is already eating him up.

And then – we aren't aware of anything happening at first, but there's a sudden movement among the line of retreating Greeks – a sort of gathering and swirling, a surging around something.

Achilles is staggering from side to side. He's swaying. The movement of men around him speeds up, acquires urgency.

And he falls, a small crumpled heap far away in the distance. Women around me gasp. I can't see Paris, but I think he's laughing now.

And then I realise what it is he's done, and how he's done it.

Chapter Thirty-two

With a huge roar, the Greeks are upon us now, a great black tidal wave of them. Trojans suddenly come out of nowhere and gather, weapons poised, shields at the ready. The war is upon us again.

I can see Paris for a while – see him talking to some of his friends. Then the crowd of men surges around him and he disappears. I imagine he's planned to beat a quick retreat at this point, but he might not be able to get out.

And then Greek force meets Trojan force, and we're back again, in the inevitable crashing and clashing and shouting and screaming, the smell of blood, the cacophony of battle. I can't bear to watch any more and go back into the palace.

It's another long day. And not until the light starts to thicken is it all over – another day of new widows and orphans and weeping, and burials.

The first thing we learn is that Achilles is dead. Is really dead. His goddess mother tried to protect him from harm when she dipped him in the Styx, but Paris found his only weak point.

The little scratch couldn't have killed him, and soon everyone's whispering *poison*. Wolfsbane, most likely, a concentrated distillation. Only a few people know how to refine poison like this.

People are confused. It's not a man's way to die, it's not a warrior's way to kill. But it's good for Troy to have Achilles dead. No one here mourns him.

Except me. I don't know why, but I admired him, in spite of his cruelty. He was a man who wouldn't break his word, who was loyal to his friends. And there was something about him – I don't normally see much in men, but I could understand why Briseis loved him and was true to him in her heart.

That isn't the only news we hear this afternoon. For Paris too is dead – tracked down ruthlessly by Philoctetes, a Greek who'd been another of Lady Helen's suitors. Paris had tried to get away, but the Greeks were too quick for him. He fought back, but in his stupid armour he didn't stand a chance. Before he died, he was heard to call out, 'Tell Helen I was brave! Tell her that!'

Poor Paris. For he brought down the greatest of heroes, in what may have been the most skilful move of his life, and yet no one's giving him credit for it. Just a sheer fluke, some say. Apollo obviously had a hand in guiding that arrow, say others.

No one seems to be contented with the result. Even enemies of Achilles seem disappointed that it wasn't a proper 'heroic' death. But I don't know. I've seen too many deaths recently, and I start to think that there's no such thing. Heroes are better alive.

We slaves gather in the great kitchens this evening whispering furtively to each other. We don't know how the King and Queen are taking the death of yet another son. Only Deiphobus is left now. And Helenus. But Helenus is nowhere to be seen – he's vanished into nowhere. Some people say he's been captured, others whisper that he's defected. Nobody knows.

What everyone wants to know is how Lady Helen is taking the death of her husband. Her chamber door is firmly shut. There are only two attendants with her, old Aethra and another younger woman whom she's fond of. There are no sounds coming from the room, no weeping, no wailing. As always, Lady Helen is an enigma.

And I wonder whether Priam will still talk of her as his 'dear daughter' now she's taken away yet another of his sons. All these deaths, and for what? Their great love story is over now, buried with Paris in the dust.

And Paris will be buried, too, put in a hole in the ground like any poor man whose family can't afford the funeral rites. There can be no more funeral pyres on this treeless plain. Probably the Greeks will burn the corpse of Achilles tonight, even if they have to destroy some of their ships to find the wood, probably they will lay his bones next to his beloved Patroclus. He'll have a hero's burial, at least.

The next few days pass in a kind of haze for us all, as the palace tries to come to terms with all of these deaths. The Greeks are quiet too, in their camp by the sea. Some people say that they're tired of the war and will go home, but I don't believe that. There are also rumours that crafty Odysseus is ordering something be built – under wraps so no one can see what it is. But it's big. An offering to the gods, some people guess. But I fear it's something more sinister than that.

And Achilles's son has arrived at last – Pyrrhus. He's

full of fury at his father's death. Though what did he imagine Achilles had come to Troy for? It surprises me that men can kill, and then be angry with others for killing. No doubt Pyrrhus will avenge his father in a terrible way – then his victims will avenge in their turns. There must be a better way of resolving things than killing – all this war.

But women have no choice but to put up with what men decide for them, it seems.

And as days pass, it seems that even Lady Helen – remote and beautiful Lady Helen – has more to put up with than her lover's death. It's the custom here that an unmarried man will marry his brother's widow – it's to protect her and save her from destitution.

But guess what – shrewd Deiphobus has decided that it's his duty to marry Lady Helen now. Paris isn't here to stop him, Hector isn't here – Priam is beyond caring. Deiphobus has the most beautiful woman in the world all to himself. Some of us whisper unkindly that he didn't feel obliged to do his duty to Andromache when she was widowed. Andromache is pleasant-looking, but probably no one would go to war for her.

And how does Lady Helen feel, being bargained over and passed round among her brothers-in-law? I only see her once over these days, and that's when she's being taken, veiled, to my goddess's temple to take part in a simple, war-time marriage ceremony with Deiphobus, no feasting, no dancing, no garlands. He looks smug. She – on the way back, with her veil flung back – is pale, aloof, somewhere miles away. But also, in a strange way, determined. Lady Helen is planning something.

Chapter Thirty-three

I notice the beggar in the lower town when I'm on my way to do an errand for one of the kitchen slaves. I'm conscious of beggars now, ever since I saw the divine Apollo that day. There aren't many beggars in Troy now – there isn't a lot to beg for. This one is hobbling up the hill, dressed in filthy rags that barely cover him, his face scabbed and scarred, ingrained with dirt, eyes squinting and gummed up. I do notice something strange about him, as I pass. A beggar like that should stink – yet this one doesn't. I turn to look, bewildered, for a moment as he trudges up the hill towards the Scaean Gate. I wonder, briefly, what he wants – but then, Eto calls out to me from the doorway of his food shop. He's got a consignment of salt – the cooks have been short of salt for weeks. A bargain has been made, but Eto isn't happy. He wants more. I tell him I'm just a messenger, in no position to bargain. We argue. He's getting cross and quite nasty. I snap back at him, though really I don't care. It's unlikely that any fine food will get back to us slaves – we've been living on barley gruel for weeks now.

But by the time I trudge up the hill, carrying a jar of salt – smaller than the cook wanted – I'm feeling quite cross and I've forgotten about the beggar who didn't smell. I have a row to come with the cook, who'll be angry with me in turn. We're all a bit short-tempered these days.

Later that afternoon, I'm drifting about the palace, trying to look busy, when a small boy slave comes up to me, and whispers that Lady Helen wants to see me. I let out a sigh of exasperation, hoping I'm not being sent to buy more poison, but I recollect myself when I realise that since I spoke to her last, Lady Helen's world has fallen apart. When I knock at her door, I'm feeling quite nervous about what I might find, and what I might be asked to do.

Lady Helen opens it for me herself, which is strange. Neither of her slaves is present, and nor, I'm glad to see, is her new husband. Her heavy hair has been pulled back, and fastened with pins at her neck. She wears a plain robe of fine unbleached wool, tied at the waist with a dark sash. She looks tired, with violet circles under her beautiful eyes; and her lips are tight. There is still that guarded, secretive look to her. You will never get to know what Lady Helen is thinking. Maybe it's because of her divine father – having a god for a parent makes someone different in all sorts of ways – their actions aren't accountable in the way that the rest of us are accountable. The weird determination with which she left her family, and hazarded a whole city with her leaving. The way Achilles enacted revenge upon revenge on Hector – I think of the contrast between his murderous rage, and his courtesy. It's as though the half-divine are acting out a story in their lives, a story that follows hidden rules, weaves patterns that we, wholly mortal, can't see. Maybe one day, the pattern will be revealed, the story made clear. But not yet. Not now.

She gives me a little smile. 'Good,' she says softly. 'Come in.'

At first I think the room is empty, then I see the man

172

sitting on a stool in a dark corner. 'Madam! What's he doing here?'

For it is the scabby beggar from the lower town. At my words he gets up from the stool, and I notice the beggar's crouch slowly straightening up, the eyes unsquinting. He smiles, to show white perfect teeth. His eyes twinkle. He's not tall, but he's powerful. And whoever he is, he's no beggar.

'So this is the young lady,' he says in perfect Greek. 'You think she'll help?'

'Of course she'll help,' says Lady Helen. 'She's Greek, like you.'

'And like *you*, Lady Helen.'

'Eirene, this is Odysseus, King of Ithaca and an old friend of mine.'

Odysseus, famous for being the Greek King's advisor and one of the most cunning men anywhere. I can't think of anything to say, and my mouth must have fallen open, for the man gives a hearty laugh.

'And so what is the King of Ithaca doing in my Lady's bedchamber, in the middle of the enemy, you're thinking, aren't you, miss?'

Well, yes, I was thinking just that. I still can't find words.

'Odysseus has come here for a reason. Now he needs your help.'

Now, I'm not a Trojan, but the Greeks have been the enemies of my city for years, and I'm not sure I like the sound of this.

'You want me to *spy*, my Lady?'

'No,' says the man, quickly. 'I don't expect you to spy.

I just need you to show me a way out of this city. Lady Helen says you know all the secret routes.'

He's holding something wrapped in a cloth of oiled linen, about the length of a man's forearm. 'What's that, sir?'

'Oh nothing. Just an old bit of wood, no use to anyone.'

Well, no one's going to risk coming into an enemy city for a bit of old rubbish. But you can't say that to a king.

Lady Helen gives a tinkling little laugh. 'I don't think she believes you, dear Odysseus.'

And at that moment I realise what it is he's taken. Oh, I don't like this. I don't like getting caught up in Lady Helen's snarls – it feels like being trapped in a spider's web.

'That's not just a bit of old wood, sir.'

'No. But I have good reason to take it.'

'The goddess will be angry.'

'On the contrary. The goddess wishes me to take it.'

I look hard at him. I remember I've heard it said that this man, cunning and wily, is particularly favoured by my goddess. I can't understand why, but the gods have their reasons.

'Sir, you didn't…you didn't hurt the priestess, did you?'

'Certainly not. I would never harm her priestess, even in an enemy city. No, I found a time when the temple would be empty. She takes a little nap in the afternoon, I believe.'

Well, I believe she does. But how did he know that?

I look from one to the other, still unsure what to say. I'm standing in front of the open window, when Odysseus gives a gasp.

174

'What did you say your name was, girl?'

'Eirene.'

But he's not looking at me; he's looking at something behind me. I turn, but it's already flown away. A little owl with yellow eyes, sitting on the window sill. Lady Helen hasn't seen; she's walked over to a chest, and taken something out.

'Look, Odysseus, do you remember this?'

It's a silver cup, patterned with vine leaves. But Odysseus's eyes are still on that empty window sill. He turns to look briefly at what Lady Helen holds. 'Yes, I remember,' he says, shortly. 'Feast at your palace. You served me wine in it, as I remember.'

'How long ago those days seem now,' murmurs Lady Helen. She's lost in a reverie of her own now. Which gives the King of Ithaca a good chance to stare at me.

'Perhaps I shall take two things from the city of Troy,' he says, very quietly. I go cold.

Then suddenly there's a knocking at the door. 'Open up, my Lady!' shouts the voice of a guard. Lady Helen and Odysseus exchange looks. In a trice he's hidden under her bed, and she's draped a blanket over the bed so he can't be seen.

Then she goes and answers the door. If it's taken a longer time than usual, then everyone knows the Lady Helen never does things in a hurry.

'Yes?' she says coolly.

The guard apologises. But there's been an intruder in the palace; someone's killed a guard to get in. The man must be found. His eyes rake over the room – but he sees nothing untoward, and he doesn't dare burst in.

'How terrible. I do hope you find him,' she says, as she closes the door. Odysseus comes out from his hiding place.

'You killed a man,' says Lady Helen. 'That was bad of you.' But she doesn't sound very worried. 'Eirene is very loyal to her mistress, the Lady Cassandra. But all you want to do is to get out of here, isn't that so, Odysseus? You aren't going to harm anyone else, are you?'

'Not today. I promise you that. I just need some help getting out of here.'

'However did you get in?' I ask.

'Luck,' says the King of Ithaca with a grin. 'But luck doesn't work twice.'

'Do as he says,' says Lady Helen.

Well, I don't see why I should. But then suddenly, just as I heard them in the temple, the words seem to form themselves inside my head, *Do as he says. I shall look after you...*

If it's my task to help him, then I shall. The grey blanket is still draped over the bed, and it gives me an idea.

'You can stop being a beggar and become an old woman,' I say. Some of the old widows in Troy still cover themselves up and veil their faces. Lady Helen sees what I mean, and together we drape the blanket right around the King of Ithaca, covering his face and beard. Just his eyes peer out, looking bemused. Lady Helen fastens the cloak with a bronze pin and stands back to admire her work. She gives a little giggle. 'Just don't stride, Odysseus, dear. Take little tiny steps. Oh, I wish I could see you hobbling down the streets of Troy!'

We leave Lady Helen's room, and creep down the

corridor. I'm going to take him down my quiet back way, the stairs that go down near the privies.

We're just level with the privy door, when I hear footsteps and loud voices round the bend of the corridor. Men are coming.

Without thinking, I open the door of the privy and shove the King of Ithaca inside.

When the two guards burst into view, there's just a girl, hanging on to the privy door, and jumping up and down.

'Have you seen anyone? Seen a man?'

'What? Ooh, hurry *up*, Marya.'

'Who's in there?'

'Marya. She's got the runs. And I think I have too. Hurry up!'

'We heard there's been an intruder. You've not seen anyone?'

'No! Oooh!'

'Well, if you see him, tell us.'

And then they're gone. The corridor is silent. Cautiously I open the privy door.

'You can come out now.'

He grins at me. 'The runs, indeed! I couldn't have lied better myself!'

I don't smile back. I've saved his skin – not quite sure why – but I'm not ready to be friendly with him. 'Come on. We'll go down these stairs. Careful, it's dark.'

And he follows me down. We emerge in a quiet corner of the courtyard, and the little back door that's seldom locked.

The citadel is quiet today. But I still have to hiss at

him to remember to hobble as he walks behind me. I'm taking him to the west gate as that leads straight on to the plain without going through the lower city. I want him out of here as quickly as possible. I don't know the guards on duty, which is a relief. I tell them that my old aunt wants to visit her husband's grave. The guard gives us a cursory look and reminds me that the gates will be shut in a couple of hours. I push the veiled bundle through in front of me, and we're out on the plain.

I've no intention of going any further. 'You can go now, sir,' I say. 'Just keep hobbling till you're out of sight.'

'Come with me, little Eirene,' he says. 'You'll see how I repay my debts.'

Does he think I'm mad? As if I'd go off to the Greek camp, to men who trade women around like toys. For a moment, I think he's going to take my arm and try and drag me, but he'd be foolish to do this so close to the walls. So he hobbles off. 'I won't forget you,' is the last thing he says. I hope he does.

It's not until I go back to the city – through a different gate – that I realise how foolish I've been, and what a risk I've taken. But now it's all worked out well, I discover I've quite enjoyed this afternoon's little adventure.

Chapter Thirty-four

Cassandra leans out of her window, and calls down into the courtyard that people should leave the city now, should escape. She tells them that they'll be burned, slaughtered, raped, enslaved. People go to Deiphobus who's now acting as ruler, and complain. It's upsetting us, they say. Please put her away. I don't know why it never occurs to people to believe what she says – but they don't.

And then I see her – she's being taken out of her chamber with the window to the courtyard, by two guards. She looks unkempt and dishevelled – pale with burning eyes. But not mad. She throws back her head as she sees me in an aristocratic gesture. 'Stop!' she says to the guards, and surprisingly they do. 'Let me go. I'm not going to run.' And they do. I go up to her, and we embrace. I can't think of anything to say to her, and I think I'm crying. She pushes me away, and wipes my eyes with the end of her scarf. 'We're never going to see each other again, you know that, don't you?'

'Yes, Cassandra, I know.' I don't realise till afterwards that I've used her name like this. A slave shouldn't address her mistress by her name. But it doesn't matter now. And I know she's right – this is the last time we'll meet.

'She'll kill me, you know,' she goes on. 'But it's all right. I'll be better off dead. And she'll kill him too – bah! Monster, he deserves it...'

179

Who's 'she'? Who, out of all the candidates in this bloody war, is the 'monster'? I can't follow her. But I know, because the god has taken hold of her, that she's right.

Then she turns to her guards. 'What are you staring at? You'll be dead too, you know. For what it's worth. Go on, then, take me to my new prison.'

And they're off, to a little room tucked away behind the wine stores, where no one can hear her cry out.

She has a mother, she has a father. Why aren't they looking after her?

When I remember that last evening of celebration in the great hall, King Priam sitting upright and proud in his great chair, silver hair glittering, Queen Hecuba still and dignified, Hector laughing and telling stories of valour, Lady Helen entering in a cloud of beauty, the musician singing, the slaves hastily stuffing bits of the copious banquet into their mouths. When I remember all that, and see how things are now – Priam simply an old man, Deiphobus fast turning into an ineffectual tyrant, the cupboards bare, young widows going about their business with pursed lips, the dusty wind blowing up empty streets – it feels as though they were two quite different cities. Even if the war ended tomorrow, Troy has lost all its greatness, all its splendour.

But how much longer can this war last? The rumours are coming thick and fast that the Greeks are preparing to go home. And some of our allies, camped on the plain, have already rolled up their tents, saddled their horses and gone back to their own lands. The summer is nearly over now, and the fighting days are numbered. But somehow, I don't think we've seen the last of the war.

It's one of those days that we see often at Troy – no sun, and that dry and dusty wind blowing everywhere, making everyone uncomfortable. Everything is a struggle. And for me, things take a sharp downhill turn when the King's steward, whom I've been avoiding, catches me looking out of a window. He tells me sharply that I don't have enough to do here, and I'm to report tomorrow morning to the supervisor by the washing pools. I'm to become a laundry slave – one of the things I feared worst. Apart from the drudgery, the washing pools are dangerous places to work – many girls have been killed or taken off by stray Greeks. Finally, I've run out of chances.

It's the afternoon now – someone gives me another errand. I'm to go down to the town and collect some kitchen knives that have been repaired by the tinsmith just outside the gates. It's make-do-and-mend, these days in the palace – a few years ago old knives would just have been thrown on the rubbish heap, but things have to be made to last.

But I never get down as far as the walls. For as I cross the courtyard, someone I don't know runs up to me and says I have to call in at the Branch of Hyssop – something to collect for Her Ladyship. Lady Helen, I guess he means, but doesn't say. I wonder that Lady Helen hasn't asked me herself, but I don't waste much time thinking about it. The bundle of knives is only a small one – I can easily do both things.

I notice that there's a mule cart tethered in the narrow lane outside the Branch of Hyssop. I go through the leather door curtain into the herb scented darkness and look for Myron. He comes in from his little back room holding a cloth in his hands. He seems to be wearing his travelling gear, boots, cape and woollen hat. For some reason, at that moment, I take in everything in the little shop, the chafing dishes on bronze tripods, the terracotta jars on shelves, the bundles of dried herbs. Myron sees me looking around, and gives his nasty, sharp-toothed grin. 'You just never know, do you?' he says, 'When you're looking at something for the last time.'

And then suddenly, he's come round behind me and before I can escape, has pinned my arms behind my back and is pressing the cloth against my mouth and nose. It smells pungent, overwhelming, and makes me dizzy. My eyes sting, my limbs are heavy, and a buzzing darkness breaks over me.

When I regain consciousness, I find I've been trussed up like a chicken. My arms are tied, my legs are tied at the knee and at the feet, there's a gag over my mouth. I'm lying under a smelly blanket, on bare splintery wood, and bumping up and down. I'm in the mule cart, rattling down the uneven paved streets of the city. There's a jarring halt and I hear men's voices, and Myron's voice saying in reply, 'Oh nothing. Just some sacks of barley for the lads in the Dardanian camp.'

I try to shout, but I can't; try to move, but he's trussed me up so well...

I think we must be passing through the gates of the lower city and out into the plain.

Fear kicks in – I can't believe this is happening to me, that I was so foolish as to let it happen. My mind runs through all the things that might be going on – and none of them are good.

In the suffocating darkness, I lose all sense of time and place. As the cart lurches and bumps I try to tie in what I can feel with the geography of things – are we going towards the distant hills, or down to the sea? I just can't tell.

And after a while, I stop struggling. Whatever is happening to me – this is my fate. My thread is being woven this way. I remember what my friend said to me in the slave ship – better just to stay quiet. So that's what I do. I pray to my goddess that she'll look after me. After all, whatever happens to me, it can't be much worse than scrubbing clothes against the rocks in the icy river.

Chapter Thirty-five

The cart comes to a lurching halt. I hear voices. The cart jolts as the driver gets down. More voices. I can't hear what they're saying, but I think they're talking in Greek.

He's back on the cart again. Now the cart seems to be twisting and turning as it drives through spaces too narrow to be taking a cart. People swear at the driver – he swears back. The old familiar sounds of the Greek language make their ways through my ears – it's oddly comforting, in spite of everything.

And then eventually, the cart comes to a halt. More voices. More comings and goings. Someone seems to be shouting for someone else to be fetched. '...be here soon,' I hear. Greek. The language of my long-ago childhood.

And then suddenly light floods in on me. The smelly blankets are flung back, and I'm looking up at the hot white sky. And then the stink of the Greek camp. So it was Myron who has been spying for the Greeks all this time. Not much of a surprise there.

I hear a familiar voice, 'Holy Zeus, man, I didn't mean you to bundle her up like a pig on a griddle! Get her out of that, at once.'

Someone scrambles into the cart, helps me first to my knees, and unties the gag, then cuts through the bonds on my arms and ankles. I'm stiff and trembling and dizzy when he helps me to my feet, and out of the back of the cart. My knees shake and I don't think they're going to support me. Dazzling circles spin across my eyes.

I'm aware of a press of people. Men. Crowding all around, so I can see nothing beyond them.

But then I gather myself together, stand up straight, and look into the eyes of a man, stocky, dark, twinkling-eyed, white smile. He wears a robe of good linen, and gold earrings. He looks like a friendly pirate.

He also looks a little like a scabby beggar whom I saw not long ago.

He reaches out as if to take my hand, but I snatch it from him. 'My dear, miss,' he says. 'Do let me apologise for that undignified arrival. When I told my uncouth friend that you were to be brought here, I meant it to be done in a civilised way.'

I can hear Myron starting to protest in the background. 'But my lord, I had to, she wouldn't have...' Someone shuts him up.

I find my voice. What comes out of my mouth is in Greek, as though I'd never been away. 'How dare you bring me here like this! What do you mean by it? I don't belong to you. I belong to King Priam.'

King Odysseus smiles at me and gives a little bow. 'No, miss, you belong to nobody now. You are no longer a slave. You are free.'

My mouth falls open in mid-tirade. The words I've so longed to hear; but I still don't trust this man. He puts a hand around my shoulder, and ushers me towards the open door of a wooden building. We pass through the crowds of men. I glimpse a city of tents, with somewhere in the distance, masts. And a great strange dark shape that I can't yet make out.

The wooden building seems to be a lodge like the one they built for Achilles, though they haven't finished this one off so beautifully. There is straw on the floor, a couple of crude wooden tables, stools, braziers and some bronze lamp-stands. Armour and spears are bundled into one corner, with a pile of battered wooden chests.

Three or four men are standing over a table. There's a shallow terracotta dish filled with sand. A broad man with a heavy, dark face is tracing lines in the sand – it seems to be some sort of plan – while the others, a man with foxy ginger hair, and an old man, nearly as old as Priam, lean over him, and are making comments.

They look up as Odysseus and I enter the hall. The big dark man says, 'Still sorting out that secret business of yours, Odysseus?'

'This won't take me long,' he says. 'Then I'll be with you.'

'It better hadn't,' snaps the dark man. He looks at me curiously. He wears a good tunic of crimson wool with patterned borders. There's a gold ornament around his neck. The red-haired man and he look very similar in spite of their colouring. They are brothers. I realise who it is I'm looking at.

The other side of the story. King Agamemnon and his brother Menelaus. Agamemnon, who sacrificed his own daughter for a favourable wind, who tried to keep Chryseis from her father, and who stole Briseis from Achilles. Menelaus, who brings a whole army to revenge his faithless wife. The pursuers. The men who are trying to destroy us.

The woollen curtain on the door flaps aside, and in strides Achilles.

My heart stops still for a moment, and then I realise it's not Achilles. He's very like him, but he's younger and taller, and his wiry fair hair isn't a mass of curls. He says, 'I've been checking the arrows, sir, and we have plenty. Not so many bows, but there should be enough if we manage them properly.'

Pyrrhus. Meaning 'fair-haired' – the golden-haired son of the great dead hero, just torn away from his new young wife to be here. Yet by his manner, he seems to be enjoying being here, in spite of everything. I wonder what his wife is thinking, waiting for him all alone in Phthia? I remember that she's Lady Helen's daughter – she must have conflicting feelings about this war, waged to drag Lady Helen back to her red-haired first husband.

Perhaps – who knows – Lady Helen might even prefer to go back to him, rather than being stuck with Deiphobus. He looks bad-tempered, though, the red-haired one. I wouldn't like to be his wife, or his child.

Odysseus sees me staring and pats me on the shoulder. 'Come,' he says. 'You need to hear this. There's not much time.'

He takes me to a dark corner of the hall, and points to a narrow wooden bench. I sit down, and he sits next to me.

'Before I left Ithaca,' he said, 'I had a dream. The goddess came to me, and told me she wanted two things. She wanted the ancient statue from Troy to be taken to Athens and placed in the new temple the King is building for her there. And she wanted a priestess for the temple. I was to find that priestess.'

He's goes quiet, and then I see what he's getting at. 'But…I'm not a priestess. I'm…I'm a Trojan slave.'

He shakes his head. 'No, miss, you aren't a slave any more. Whatever happens, you're free. I'll see to that. But…'

He leans forward on the bench, staring intently at his clasped hands. He's very serious now, and he looks to be like a man who doesn't care to be serious too often. 'In Lady Helen's room, the goddess's sacred bird came. She showed me who it was I was looking for; she's marked you out. That's why I sent for you.'

Whatever he says, I don't quite believe him, don't like my future being 'sorted out' like this, don't like being dragged from Troy like a sack of rubbish. 'I want to go back to Troy.'

'No, miss, you don't. You certainly don't want to go back to Troy. In a minute I'll show you why. Now, I'm going to take you to a tent where two of my men will look after you till this evening; your loyalties might make you escape, and I don't want that to happen. A small boat will leave on the evening tide. My men are going with you. They've been injured, so they're of no use in the fighting. They're taking their new wives to Pireus. And they're taking you – and you're taking the goddess's sacred statue.'

I can't take all of this in. I'm aware that something momentous is happening to me, but I can't make any sense of it. From the across the room, Agamemnon calls out to Odysseus. 'Come on, man! You're needed over here! Sort out that business of yours quickly, will you?'

Odysseus stands up. When I hesitate, he says, 'You don't have a choice.'

The faces of the men round the table stare at me indifferently. Odysseus strides towards the door. No, I don't really have a choice. I follow him.

Out into the stink and clamour of the Greek camp. Something's definitely going on – men are rushing hither and thither, shouting out to others, carrying armour, spears, helmets. Then I see the great dark *thing* that I'd noticed before. What is it? It's as high as a house, a great black shape. There's a turret at the top, and a huge wooden pole sticking out at the front like an animal's head. It seems to be made of wood and covered with hides. As I watch, men are climbing all over it, and sloshing buckets of water over the hides and wood.

'What is *that*?'

He gives a harsh little laugh. 'That, dear miss, is why you don't want to go back to Troy. By tomorrow night, Troy will be no more.'

I can't bear this. 'No, no, please no.'

'Oh, there's nothing you can do; the plan is already underway. But before it happens, I want my goddess to know that I haven't forgotten her – that her statue is on its way to Athens. With you. Come along, now, I've got no more time to waste.'

Well, I follow him. To a little tent, where two men sit outside and guard me, but with great politeness, until the sky darkens.

And so it happens, that as evening falls, I'm in a small fishing boat, just half a dozen sailors, two Greek soldiers (one has an injured arm, the other a damaged knee), their captured Trojan women – who don't seem at all unhappy, I have to say – various bundles of war booty, a statue no bigger than a man's forearm wrapped in oiled linen, making my way across a dark sea, into more darkness – and towards what?

A Year Later

'Mint, do you think?' says one of the old ladies, sitting in the scented shade of a great bay tree. 'With a little honey?'

'That sounds very nice, dear. Mint is very soothing.'

'A little mint, Eirene? Would you?'

It's not a command. A year ago it would have been a command – now it's just a request among friends – a young woman better able to do bending and gathering herbs than old bones can manage.

It's quiet here in the shade of the little walled garden next to the priestess's house, here high on the rocky hill. There are bay trees and fruit trees, evergreen ilexes and climbing white roses. Marjoram, thyme and a dozen other herbs grow in the neat beds. I'm weeding the beds because I don't really want to sit with the two old ladies in the shade talking about their youth, kind though they are.

Not far away, though, we can hear the sounds of building. If I looked over the wall, I could see the builders, running up and down their wooden ladders, scrambling over scaffolding, with piles of terracotta roof tiles. The new temple will be finished soon, and then the ancient statue that's been waiting here in a secret hiding place can be put before the altar, for the Athenians to revere.

One of the old ladies is Eritha, priestess of Athene. I didn't believe her when I arrived when she said she'd never see another winter after this one – but I can see her death on her now, her limbs wasted, her eyes big and shadowed in her old face. But she's happy enough, and not in too much pain. The goddess is looking after her, and soon, she says, she'll walk in the flower-scented meadows of the blessed.

The other old lady is familiar to me. I've seen her over the years, always sitting in her chair, dozing off. She's Aethra, who was a slave to the Lady Helen. Only now do I find out her story and discover that she was actually the mother of King Theseus, the old King of Athens. She was enslaved years ago, and now in turn, she's been rescued by her grandson, and her grandson is Demophon, King of Athens, who dines with us one night in four, and the gilded finials of whose palace I can just see from where I kneel by the bed of mint.

When we first came to Athens, word had got out of the arrival of the goddess, and there were crowds out to meet us, throwing flowers before us. Wrapped in my travelling cloak, over my Trojan slave-costume, I felt bewildered by all the adulation as we made our way by mule cart from the harbour at Pireus to the great acropolis at Athens. I was made even more unhappy, the night of our arrival, when the great beacon blazed on Mount Hymettus – one of the chain that announced to the jubilant Greeks that at last Troy had indeed fallen.

Eritha was very kind to me that evening – but I don't think she quite understood why I should feel so sad that the city where I'd been enslaved for so many years was no more. 'You must be pleased, dear; chosen by the goddess, you'll be a great lady. When I'm gone, you'll be priestess in Athens, and kings will come to you for your advice, and you'll have everything you could ever need.' Then she put her arm on my shoulder. 'Don't cry,' she said. 'It's over. Your nightmare is over.'

But it wasn't. Not for many months. And it isn't over now, though I keep it to myself, and try to put on a smiling face for the goddess.

As the news began to trickle out, the nightmare got worse. For Troy really was taken – by the great ugly monstrous creature the Greeks had built. In the dark of night, they wheeled it to the walls of Troy – yes, they knew about the weakened section in the wall by the old fig tree. They used the great log in front to batter away at the walls. The wet hides they'd covered the monster with kept it from being burned; the great log rammed and rammed, until eventually the walls were breached, and the Greeks rushed in.

I still can't bring myself to think of all that happened next; Priam's great palace overrun, everything stripped and smashed and burned. The great towers burned – just as I saw them in my dream. All my old friends among the slaves – where are they now? Priam is dead – killed before the altar of the god Apollo, who'd long since ceased to look after his loyal people. Deiphobus dead, and all of Priam's other sons, I think. Hecuba was taken, but managed to jump from the boat she was in and drowned. Andromache was taken – by Achilles's golden-haired son, as his concubine. What humiliation for her – and what a gift for Pyrrhus's wife. As for little Astyanax – I don't know. Some people say he was killed – hurled from the walls of Troy so he wouldn't live to avenge his father's death. But others say no, he wasn't killed, and that an old retainer managed to smuggle him out of the city. It's said that Aeneas escaped, and so did Glaucus. Helenus has somehow turned up in Greece, with Pyrrhus. Did he turn traitor in the end and betray his people? I don't know the truth of that – but it would answer questions that I've never found an explanation for – for example, just how did Odysseus find his way through the palace and into Lady Helen's room? And how did he know that the Temple of Pallas Athene was likely to be left unlocked and unattended during the afternoon? Odysseus set off for Ithaca with his twenty ships – he hasn't arrived home yet, but everyone says he must have been blown off course and will turn up any day now. You don't keep someone like Odysseus down.

But there's one last thing, the worst thing of all.

For when the women of Troy were parcelled out among their captors, Agamemnon took Cassandra. What she must have suffered from those big pawing hands of his I can't imagine. Yet we hear from Mycenae, that as soon as he arrived, his doting wife, who'd taken a lover in his absence, murdered him. They say she'd never forgiven her husband for sacrificing their daughter. But also, she killed Cassandra who had done her no harm. My mistress died, as she knew she was going to. Poor darling – I hope it was quick for her, at the end.

And what of Lady Helen, the beautiful cause of all this carnage? Why, she's back home in Sparta, with her first husband Menelaus, calm and happy and beautiful as ever, so people who've visited say. Apparently he burst into her chamber, prepared to kill her, but she knelt down before him so prettily, so repentant. She even bared her breast for his dagger – and that did the trick. He remembered her beauty and couldn't bring himself to kill her. Now she's queen again, in her old palace, as though the last few years have never happened.

All those years of war – all that slaughter. And in the end, for what? Agamemnon went home with his ships laden with Trojan treasure, but he never lived to enjoy it. A fine and civilised city destroyed. So many people killed. So many heroes dead. So many women enslaved and raped. And it doesn't seem to me that in the end anyone, Greek or Trojan is better off for it. Maybe war is always like that. There can be no winners.

Except, perhaps, and thanks to the mysterious favour of the goddess, myself. I'm no longer a slave. All the important people of the city come to me so that they can ask favours of the goddess. This city is dedicated to her, and I know she'll be kinder than Apollo was to Troy. I'm learning all the things a priestess must learn, before Eritha dies. I'm young for a priestess, I know that, but no one seems to mind – everyone feels I've been chosen. I have my own chamber in the priestess's house, and I'm waited on by a little slave, a girl from Lycia. At first I tried to tell her I didn't want a slave, that she could serve me as a free person – but she grew upset at that and thought it meant that I was casting her off. So she stays here as a slave for the while, but perhaps when she's older and wants to marry, then I shall give her her freedom and a dowry.

While the new temple is being built, I perform the goddess's ceremonies in the old wooden shrine – just a circle of wooden pillars and a flat altar. I bring her wine, honey and oil, morning and evening. Often I pray to her to look after Cassandra's sad little spirit – Cassandra whose own god abused her so, should have a friend in the afterlife. I hope she hears me.

There's usually a train of people coming up the hill, who want to ask her favours. They'll bring their own sheep and goats to sacrifice, and the smoke of the fires rises as it should. Maybe my goddess is one who prefers sweet wine and oil to blood – but that's just how I feel.

When I first arrived, I was shy and scared at the thought of serving her myself, but Eritha was patient and I think I learn quickly and now the routines come easily to me. When the great new temple is built, we'll have to choose three or four more girls of good family to act as minor priestesses and to help me with the ceremonies. I'll have to train them myself, if Eritha is no longer with us, but I think I can do that now. My goddess will help me as she always has done. She is kind to her followers, sometimes in strange ways. After Odysseus had stolen the statue from the temple, Deiphobus chose to blame Theano, and banished her to serve in another temple, outside Troy, far away beyond the hills. She left weeping – but now, I imagine, as she hears what's happened to the rest of the women of Troy, she must be rejoicing that she's been spared.

I've never seen my goddess – she hasn't chosen to appear as cruel Apollo did – and in a way that pleases me. But often I can feel her behind me guiding my thoughts. If she has granted me the Sight, it's never a curse, as it was with Cassandra.

Sometimes, at twilight, I think I see a grey shape gliding through the trees, or a little owl perching on the branches staring at me. This is my life now; I'm happy here. And though I'll never stop thinking about Cassandra and Troy, the nightmares are less vivid now, the memories less painful.

Many sailors come up the long road from the harbour at Pireus to ask favours of the goddess, for she is kind to seafaring men. With their tanned faces and wide smiles, they're also my good friends. They spend all their days going up and down the coasts and in and out of all the islands.

Soon I shall set one of them in his travels to ask if anyone in the islands remembers a child called Eirene, and how she was snatched one day years ago, by pirates...

For more about Frances Thomas and her books,
visit her website at www.francesthomas.org

You can read more of The Girls of Troy trilogy in
Book 1: *Helen's Daughter*
Book 3: *Electra*

Lightning Source UK Ltd.
Milton Keynes UK
UKOW02f0801280415

250479UK00001B/13/P